Saint in Vain

Saint in Vain

By
MATTHEW K. PERKINS

RESOURCE *Publications* · Eugene, Oregon

SAINT IN VAIN

Resource Publications
An Imprint of Wipf and Stock Publishers
199 W. 8th Ave., Suite 3
Eugene, OR 97401

www.wipfandstock.com

PAPERBACK ISBN: 978-1-5326-0882-7
HARDCOVER ISBN: 978-1-5326-0883-4
EBOOK ISBN: 978-1-5326-0884-1

Manufactured in the U.S.A.   05/22/18

For Hailey

The Dead Bury Their Dead

He didn't look like much, the saint. And he wasn't. His suit fit him poorly and, now that it was soaked, its cheap polyester material clung wetly to his extremities and he appeared a sorry sight to the other funeral goers. He squinted against the soggy sunlight that leaked its way through the rain clouds and into his eyes as if designed to irritate him. Their attire was as black as their sunglasses, which they periodically removed to clear the water beads off of the plastic lenses. Where they had taken a sidewalk up the cemetery's steep hill, he opted for the sloping grass, and, after he slipped, his pant knees were splotchy and grass stained. He wondered how it could be rainy and sunny at the same time. He recalled once hearing that an average cumulus cloud weighs nearly one million pounds. There were no chairs set upon the cemetery lawn, and so the turn-out braced themselves against the cold rainfall and the death inside of both coffins.

Strange to him that they should just lay in their boxes. Strange that only eleven people came to mourn the two titans of his life.

He stood alone between the two oversized portraits of the cold departed, and as the rain continued to fall he wondered if the water would ruin the giant photos. Would the ink start to run? It hadn't started yet. And, as the pastor began reading passages from the Bible, he wondered what he was supposed to do with the glossy pictures after today—they were impractically large and they looked nothing like the two people as they were now.

Rain ran off his face the same as it ran off the lacquered wood of the coffins, and there was no telling if he cried. He held nothing in his hands and so they remained clasped in front of him or held to his eyes in order to grant a brief reprieve from the sunlight. For a moment he tried putting them in his pockets but then quickly removed them. He had never worn so much black. The lawn was soft and aerated and it made deep sucking noises under the pressure of his heels. Their graves were cut neatly into the earth and before each casket was lowered, the pastor asked him if he would like to say any words. His cheeks pinched vertically as he tried to look at the attendees through the sun rays. He raised his left hand to act as a visor to his eyes, but then he dropped it back to its clasp. Quiet in the graveyard.

He faced down the meager black mass and he said, It's times like these when we are reminded to let the dead bury their dead.

The sun prevented him from seeing the confused faces that materialized around the two caskets. Those that weren't confused only stared blankly back at him, and the pastor regarded him as if waiting for him to say more, but he didn't. He offered a solemn nod as each coffin descended into its final resting spot. The small group retreated from the hillside to the home of the saint, where faces of the newly dead looked out at them from all corners. While he chewed down a handful of crackers, his aunt asked him about what he said at the funeral, but he waved her off and disappeared into the basement of the home. No one sought him out and it wasn't long before the house was empty, all except for the soft patter of rainfall on the slatted roof. He spent the next few hours sitting in an old plush rocking chair with his baggy suit now rigid and dried around his frame. He was wondering what to do now. What now? His cat took its place on the ottoman across the room and the two stared at each other. He snapped his fingers in a gesture to call the cat over, but it only burrowed deeper into the ottoman's cushion and after a while he stopped snapping. He sat for several more hours, and when the rainfall could no longer be heard hitting the house he looked up at the ceiling in a pose of intent listening.

The cat tilted its head as it watched the saint trade his suit jacket for a sweatshirt, and then stalked him upstairs just as he slipped through the front door where his dark figure passed through the dim porch light. His head was hooded and his stern face was revealed only by the distant and intermittent flashes of lightning. The rain had stopped. He tread eastwardly in the wake of the storm and the fence-posts and hedges of yards around him seemed to have parted just for his passing. He walked to the margin of the small town, paused, and then proceeded into the seamless black outland, where the low babel of insects thickened in the rural air and a light wind twisted and bent the tall grass on each side of his path. The thunder was too distant to be heard, but within the dark clouds he witnessed arcs of lightning that lashed at the surface of the earth as if something lay buried there that might appease it. For a moment he stopped, and he studied each bolt as if it held the answer to his most important question. It was quiet, and the country was lightless except for what the lightning was willing to give. By way of a single wide paved road he climbed to the top of a hill and stilled himself against the deep night. The land to the east flattened before him and the storm continued to crawl over the crust of the earth like a purposeful, malevolent slime. In the full dark of that hill he watched—the whites of his eyes and his strange grin only made visible by the occasional flashes from the mute firmament.

Thunderhead

Seven months later he sat on the concrete steps of a small church that hardly knew of his existence, spiritual or otherwise. The steps were still damp from the spring thunderstorm the night before. Only half of the morning sun could be seen, low and rippling through the moist morning atmosphere, and he had been perched on the steps already for some time. He rubbed his hands nervously and picked at his fingernails while the plastic clacking of a boy's skateboard wheels went by on the uneven sections of concrete in front of the church.

So common was the rattle of trains here, which carted endless amounts of coal into the hungry heart of America, that the townsfolk hardly registered their sound. They were like a village at the base of a waterfall that assumes the whole world lives in a roar. But Silvio registered the metallic hum, and when a train horn came blaring over the rooftops of the neighborhood, he reflexively looked at the southern horizon where he knew it to come from. It wasn't a town that American had forgotten. It was a town that American had never known. If you were to randomly poll three adult residents, one was a government employee, one worked for the railroad, and one was unemployed. The younger generation talked incessantly about the day that they could "get out," but for every one of them that got out, there was one that stayed behind to register VIN numbers and lay train track.

Several automobiles ambled by on the street. He stood up to stretch his legs and he threw his arms to each side of his body and as he was sitting back down a large, white pickup chugged its way up to the intersection in front of the church. It towed a steel trailer with large breath holes that was designed for moving large farm animals. Even over the loud introduction of the truck, he could hear the anxious snorting and shifting hooves of the animal within. Silvio tilted his head to try to get a better look into the

4

trailer, but the truck lurched away in a stream of black exhaust smoke and he was again left alone on the stairs. He tapped his foot and continued to rub his hands together.

Four blocks away from Silvio, an old man shuffled through quiet side streets and neighborhoods marked by the homogenous presence of single floor houses with modest three-step stoops and concrete-fiber sidings that came in no more than five different pastel colors. He appeared satisfied with the quality of the morning. The storm from the night before could be witnessed in the healthy green lawns that pervaded the neighborhoods on his way to the church, and though he commuted every day, he hardly ever took the same route twice. He preferred to wander and reroute himself until his legs were beset by a satisfying fatigue. The church itself sat near the eastern edge of the shallow valley that cradled the small town. When the old man had wandered to the content of his legs, he was surprised to reach his destination and find an otherwise familiar figure sitting on the building's front steps.

Silvio?

The young man looked up from his spot on the steps. He stood up as the old man approached. Good morning, he said.

The old man placed a gentle hand on Silvio's back as they entered the front doors and said, What are you doing here? You should be at work, no?

I quit.

You quit?

Silvio nodded.

The church occupied the corner of its city block in an understated fashion—a rectangle building surrounded by a sea of grass on three sides, and a spacious parking lot on the fourth. It had no statues, no fountains, and a steeple just pronounced enough to be defined as such. The nave of the church consisted of sixteen pews set in two rows and a pulpit that fit better at the front of a classroom than a sanctuary. The two took a seat in a row near the back. A pewter representation of the Mother Mary hung on a wall behind them.

So. You quit your job?

Last week.

Is everything okay?

It's better than it's been.

Does this have something to do with your parents?

Silvio hesitated. Then he said, No.

I'm sorry, Silvio. I didn't know you were having trouble.

Silvio waved a dismissive hand at the old man. He said, There's no trouble.

You know that you don't have to tell me anything you don't want to. But do you?

Do I what?

Have anything you want to tell me.

Silvio shrugged.

The two sat quietly for several minutes. Alone in the church. Along the side of the wall, colored sunbeams streamed through the stained glass and into the dark woven carpet. The old man rubbed the creased skin on the back of his hand with the opposite thumb and then he broke the silence with a statement.

I thought your job was a good one.

It was.

And I thought they paid you well.

They did.

So what's the problem?

Silvio scanned the church to ensure that it was empty before he said, My problem is that history doesn't remember rich men.

The old man opened his mouth to respond but he was interrupted by the sound of the church's side door opening. It was a middle-aged woman and she gave the two of them a small nod of recognition before kneeling down several rows ahead of them in the opposite section of pews. She bowed her head between the triangle formed by her two clasped hands with the support of the pew ahead of her and began to silently hiss at the church's altar. The sun rose fully now, and the new lust of rays revealed in the air of the church a swarm of small, white dust particles that seemed to move every way but down. When Silvio took a deep breath they entered into his lungs and when he exhaled a new wave of them swirled and ascended to continue their mindless drift in the still atmosphere of the small church's interior. He acknowledged none of it. When he spoke again to the old man he did so quietly and craned his neck so as to direct his voice away from the praying entrant.

He said, I want to make a contribution to the world that is *significant*. I want to do something that *feels* like something. My job did not.

The old man said, How long have you felt this way?

Silvio shook his head slightly and said, It's always been like this. It just took me awhile to realize it. I always thought I wanted those things I'm supposed to want. Like a nice job, a nice family, a nice life—all of that.

You don't want a nice life?

Silvio quietly laughed. I'd love a nice life, he said. But my nice life looks different.

How so?

I'm giving my life to God.

The old man raised both of his eyebrows. You plan to join the priesthood?

Not exactly.

I don't understand.

Silvio stopped again as the woman on the other side of the nave slowly rose to her feet. A passing car and the commotion of the outside world could be heard as the front door swung open and closed again on the dense reticence inside the church. He waited another moment before he spoke again.

I'm going to be a saint.

A what?

A saint.

The old man squinted at him and said, I don't understand.

Like Saint Patrick or Saint Michael. Like them.

The old man let out laughter from deep within his chest, but stifled it after he noticed Silvio's stone face. He said, Silvio?

Yeah.

You're being serious?

Yes.

The old man shook his head. A saint?

A saint. During Sunday school, my teacher used to give us these cards—like baseball trading cards—that would have a picture of the saint on the front and attributes on the back. She told us to use the cards to pray with. She said that we could pray for a miracle, and if a miracle happened then we could attribute it to the saint that we prayed with. I never got a miracle, but I loved to look at the back and see where they were from and what they were the patrons of and how they died and all of that. They're good people, and they're brave, and they're immortalized by the church—I want to be like that. I want to do things that are *important*. I want people to know who I am and I want them to remember me when I'm gone.

The old man rubbed his forefingers over his temples in slow and gentle circles. Silvio, he said, There are so many problems with this and I don't even know where to begin. Those saints you learned about as a child didn't do those things for their own reputations. You don't just decide to be a saint—you are called to it, by God.

I *have* been called. I've dreamt of it my whole life. I'm just now realizing the significance of that dream.

The nave darkened slightly as an errant cloud passed over the sun outside. It's minor form washed in grey the entire paltry town and empty land around it. The old man shifted uncomfortably in his seat. Silvio, he said. This is silly. There is a point when we realize that the dreams we created from childhood naiveté properly dissipate. There is no shame in being practical. I understand that imagining our former dreams can feel like failure—like we didn't carry through on what's important to us—but it is okay to let a dream die. It's only natural, my friend. Whether its sports stardom, or being a princess, or a ballet dancer, or an astronaut, or the President. Whatever. We've all longed for those occupations and achievements we determine we want long before we can even comprehend the cost of realizing them—a cost we are unwilling or unable to pay. This is easier to dismiss for some than it is for others. You may simply be finding it harder than most.

Silvio took in a deep breath and exhaled slowly. Look, he said. I'm not a prophet. I don't get the luxury of having God speak down to me from a thunderhead. I have to pick up on things more subtle than that—my dreams, my relationships, my sadness—and that's the sound of his voice. That's my thunderhead. That's what roars down to me from the heavens. I've ignored it my whole life and look where that's gotten me. I went and got a girlfriend, a college degree, another college degree, and a nice job. And all I really got was more miserable with the acquisition of each of them. Don't you see? All those endeavors failed because that's not what I was called to do. I was supposed to be a saint. I *am* supposed to be a saint.

Silvio, this dream is only in your head.

Where else are dreams?

The old man offered a subtle shake of his head and then glanced around the empty church. He pressed his hands onto his knees in order to push himself to his feet and guided himself out of the row with a hand on the wooden supports to each side. When he reached the end of the row he said,

It's only in your head, Sil.

And Silvio said, That's a powerful place to be.

There are a lot of people out there, and people can believe anything. My grandpa believed that there is a direct correlation between one's use of the words *Sir* and *Ma'am* and the quality of their character. A childhood friend of mine, Tyler, believed Batman was real three years after he knew that Santa wasn't. Sergeant First Class Murphy believed in pizza and ghosts. My first girlfriend believed that everyone has a One True Love, and my mom believed in God. Charles, our demolitions expert, believed that fired rifle cartridges held the sweetest scent in the world, to which Murphy said, *Sweeter than your girlfriend's pussy?* and Charles said, *Yes sir, sweeter than that.* My high school chemistry teacher, Mr. Clemens, believed that the entire universe was once contained in an infinitely small and hot space, and now it's all contained in an infinitely large and cold space. Private First Class Church believed that baseball is the only sport worth considering, and that a large amount of money could make him happy in spite of anything else. Jude believed in America. And me? I believe in the necessity of murder—not the evil kind of murder, but a real *good* murder.

But I didn't always believe in that. Not even when I was a professional soldier. I guess it's a new adaptation of mine, because for the longest time I didn't believe in anything. I had so many beliefs thrown at me that I'd just run and duck for cover. But ducking and running is for people like me, and I'm not the bravest man I've ever met. That title belongs to someone else—you are going to meet him too. At some point in his life he realized that beliefs needed to be grasped onto, and the more stubborn you can hold on, the better. I think of it like those games of chicken I would play as a kid. Who could hold their breath the longest? Who would stay in the haunted basement the longest? Let's both grab this piece of hot metal and whoever lets go first should be ashamed, whoever lets go last deserves a damned medal. That's what believing is.

The way I figure it, running away or holding on for dear life is about all you can do, because you can't fight beliefs—you sure as hell can't fight them. Take it from me because I've been to war, and there's nothing like war to either solidify what you believe, or bomb it back to the Stone Age. If war is good for one thing, it's that it has the awesome power of transforming trivial beliefs into crystal clear ones. And if you don't have any beliefs—like I did—then it will create them for you. It will reach down into the depths of your soul, if you believe in that kind of thing, and bring back up with it a noisy conglomeration of sorrow and dirt and violence. Then those things will never go away. They'll become a part of you. No matter how far you run and no matter what you use to cover them up, that violence and that sorrow will lurk.

Between all the gods and the theories and the alien abductions, it's about impossible to know what to believe. Some people will make it sound like that's a new problem. They'll say, *There's so much crap out there today, it's hard to know what to believe.* But I'm here to tell you that there's always been a lot a crap out there. It's nothing new. But those people love to tell you that it's new, and they love to tell you that it's new right before they tell you what you *can* believe in. They are convinced that they have figured it all out, and they want to share. However, no belief is worse than the one that needs to impose itself. That one that believes it is *the* belief. I hate that one, and so should you.

All of this confusion with beliefs started after I enlisted in the United States Army, where I was just competent enough to make it through basic training. And while other graduates were strutting around in their new uniform fits and catching up with family, I was looking for the nearest bar. Not because I had a drinking problem, but because I had nothing better to do, and because ten weeks is a long time to go without a drink. True to the spirit of America's Midwest, it's not uncommon to find yourself drinking alone at a third-rate bar when you believe you'd rather be anywhere else in the world. Like any respectable bar of its type, the lighting is poor, the music is poor, the dead heads of countless wildlife are pristine, and all of the drink specials consist of whiskey.

I don't know if it was the ten week absence, or the pride I felt in graduating basic training, but on this particular evening I found cheap whiskey lighting the fire of my blood and my sentimentalism. After five drinks too many, it just so happened that one of my fellow graduates took a bar stool next to me, still dressed in his full graduate regalia. He was a younger, dark skinned man, and at the bottom of a shot glass I found all the drunken memories of an old Native American studies elective class I took in high school. He didn't seem to share in my newfound passion for all those forgotten symbols and rituals. He ignored my questions about the medicine wheel, thunderbirds, coyote, etc. He said he didn't believe in that stuff, etc.

I was going on and on without him saying much of anything. Then, over his glass of dark beer, he finally spoke up. He came from a tribe of plains Indians, but he said that all of that stuff was bullshit to him. He told me that his great-great-great-grandfather had tried to make it in the new world by becoming a stonemason. He gave a hysterical laugh and said that his great-great-great-grandfather didn't even know that there were different types of masons. That was the kind of thing that ran in the blood of families, with secrets and crafts passed from old to young as long as the surname added up. It wasn't something you decided to take up, he said. Through their generations, his family passed an adopted and failed lifestyle. He shook his head and took another drink of his beer. Whatever stability his family had, it had was ruined by the failed masonry endeavor. He said that he hadn't seen his family in years. He quit his job in construction to join the army.

And that probably should have been the end of our conversation, but the passion and whiskey that flowed through me wasn't sedated. I spun on my barstool and I reminded him of the beauty and the power that lie in the ritual of the ghost dance. I spoke of the trickster Coyote, and how he had bravely stolen fire from the gods to give to man. I told him that Manifest Destiny and masonry could suck one. But he was fed up with my drunken rant and I knew it was time to shut up. He finished his beer and said to me, Man, I'm just here to get laid.

He said that to me and walked away. At first I just figured that this guy is just a lot like me—just trying to get away from all the noise. Trying to get away from all the beliefs. A glance at the evidence would show that he believes in drinking beer and trying to have sex with women, and that's probably good enough for a lot of people. It's not enough for me, but I do hope he got laid that night.

My encounter with that young man may not seem so remarkable on its own, but less than two years later, in a similar bar and on the eve of my combat deployment, I thought I saw him again. This time, if it was him, he sat on the other end of the bar with his dark beer while I drank quietly on my whiskey until I couldn't tell the difference between my ass and my elbow. It may seem like your classic case of pre-war over reaction, but if you ask me, it wasn't reaction enough. You must understand that before I ever set boots on enemy soil (and just before this particular night) I nearly died to a god damn *hot dog*. I'll get into that story later—just know that I'm not kidding. I was terrified. I felt doomed. I was so afraid to be in a war that by the time we got to Iraq I was literally hoping to die, just so I wouldn't be afraid anymore. That much fear for that long of time can really wear on a person. I got to the point where I was even afraid of myself. I just saw myself as one more thing that could get me killed. And so on that occasion, I drank whiskey like it was the last time, because I thought it was. And when the man with the dark beer was helping me into a taxi at the end of the night there was no talk about thunderbirds or getting laid. He said, You're going to be fine, bud. I know it.

I doubt he ever knew it, but you know what happened? Through all the haze of whiskey and fear and self-pity, I happened upon a moment of clarity and I *believed* him. For no good reason, I believed him. The next morning I began to think that maybe I was going to be okay after all. The weight on my chest lifted slightly and I felt like I could breathe again. I became convinced that that guy knew something that nobody else knew. I was sure that we happened upon each other on those two nights because he served a purpose. Never mind that I wasn't even sure it was the same guy. Never mind that. For a time it appeared that my dark beer'd stranger had changed my life. That experience did a lot for me as far as believing goes, until it was all shot and blown to hell just a handful of months later. For that brief time I was no longer running from all the noise. I wasn't quite a believer, but it was the first time I felt relaxed since the moment before I saw a plane flying into skyscraper.

The difference with me is that I was drinking on the Kool-Aid, not handing it out. That takes a different kind of person, and I don't know what to make of the people who spend their lives making the Kool-Aid. Teachers and pastors and preachers and writers and economists and journalists and politicians and prophets and theorists and scientists and all the like. They spout on and on about how this paradigm is better than that one. They end-lessly rant that such and such religious beliefs are the way to heaven, and such and such aren't. Sunnis and Shiites, democrats and republicans, whatever and whatever, Amen. They're an interesting sort, and a real dangerous one too. Are they liars? I guess if someone *really* believes in something then they aren't lying, they are just mistaken. And if they really, *really* believe it, then I suppose they have a responsibility to share it with as many people as possible. I mean, if you really believe that eating an apple a day is the secret to a long and healthy lifestyle, then wouldn't you try to tell as many people as possible? What if you believed that lowering taxes would improve the lives of everyone in a given political division? You'd push for change, right? And what if you thought that a certain group of people was a major threat to your lifestyle and to your loved ones? Would you kill them? And what if you believed in God? Plant someone who believes there is a God next to someone who believes there is not. Neither is a liar, but *one* of them is mistaken. Maybe somehow both of them are. Hell, I don't know.

So you either run away from all these beliefs, only to realize that there is no escaping them, or you gotta take your pick—just pick a set of them and hold on for dear life. And let me assure you that when you finally decide on what you believe in, it's going to feel *good*. There's going to be plenty of reasons why you settled on what you did, and they are all going to make perfect sense. Beliefs bring with them a sense of purpose and a sense of security. They make the chaos of the world seem neat and understandable, and there's going to be a bunch of little signs and events that happen that are really going to solidify each belief for you. Congratulations.

That's usually the case, anyway. For me? When I finally had to start believing, I found myself running through a small town with a high-powered rifle in one hand and a dangerous set of convictions in the other. I never pegged myself as a murderer, but that's what beliefs do to you—they mess you up. Now I know that my experience isn't a typical one, but it brings me to one more point—people will kill for their convictions.

People will kill for them if only because they believe that beliefs are worth killing for. I sure as hell believe that to call a man mistaken over something he really believes in is about the most dangerous thing you can do. He might shrug it off or he might go to war with you. I found my safety, for a time, by running from the noise. Just be sure to call it something other than "noise." Call it beliefs. Call it worldviews. Call it the heart. Call it a feeling.

My friend, call it whatever you need to, so long as you can get the hell out of the way when the war comes.

Lemonade Stand

It's a lonely place. Full of a restless claustrophobia. Half a million residents in the whole state and one wouldn't know where to find them. They hide mostly in small railroad towns that materialize every fifteen miles and vanish just as quickly as they appear, never more than a few thousand people in any of them. It's as if the entire state is the work of some cosmic accountant who has hatched a scheme to launder people. And the wind always blows. It blows on it's way in from the great plains, hits the Rocky Mountains, and blows on its way back out. So numb is any native to the wind's steady whistle that the only time they register its existence is when it stops blowing. It is said that they always walk with a slight lean. If people could be simple, it would be these people. They don't dream big because they don't dream at all. Nobody knows anybody who has ever accomplished anything. The ones that make it out never speak of it again. Things that happen fifteen miles down the highway in the next town might as well happen in California. In Western Kentucky. Each town its own planet, and each planet its own factory of isolation. The wind blows, and as it blows it's as if it carries a tune with that plays in the ear of every person there and in that tune they hear something that wrangles them into a deep, complacent state of being.

Silvio strolled through one of these towns and he heard the song of the wind. It annoyed him. Following the advice of old wisdoms, he used education as a path to a better life, and though he graduated and climbed the financial ladder, it was always unclear to him, in his own mind, how necessary or applicable any of it was in the very narrow niche of his eventual profession. He thought of his experience in higher education and the countless hours of time he spent trying to gather and twist endless strands of data in an attempt to prove that people with bigger butts are smarter, oldest siblings are perfectionists, middle children are more career oriented, the youngest siblings are the best listeners, people with long hair are more healthy, people with green eyes have better sex, Mormons have the least politically savvy minds, people with small feet are more likely to read, children who eat hummus are better at math, students who are bullied in school are twice as likely to volunteer for a non-profit organization, athletes who play soccer are less likely to be as smart as athletes who play tennis who all have a poor chance at being as smart as someone who doesn't play anything. And people who are the youngest siblings with green eyes and small feet and long hair and big butts and eat hummus and are Mormon and bullied, whom, despite having good sex and solid math skills, are empirically the least likely of any single demographic to ever become the President of the United States of America—take it or leave it.

He arrived at the church, but on his way inside, Silvio noticed the old man sitting against the outside of the building with a Bible in his hands. He said, It's a little hot out here for afternoon reading isn't it?

The old man placed a marker in his book and looked up. I'm trying to get some sun and I wasn't expecting company.

The old man took a measured glance of the neighborhood and church parking lot before saying, Where'd you park?

I didn't.

Huh?

I didn't park anywhere.

Well where's your car?

I sold it, Silvio said.

Every structure comprising the small town was set in a neat grid of city blocks cleanly framed by concrete sidewalks wide enough for the comfort of three people to walk abreast. Despite that comfort, rare was it to see anybody walking here other than the adolescents who lacked the persuasion or the power to haggle out a ride from their older siblings and parents. Although the logic of an outsider would deem it possible, if not pleasant, to walk or bike to every location in a town of its size, for those who commuted with a purpose, the next destination was just as far as the one they had just come from—the grocery store is two miles from the junior high, which is three-point-four miles from the post office, which is one-point-eight miles from the elementary school, which is two-point-six miles away from home. Downtown was dead, and no one walked its forgotten pavement except for the ghosts of grandparents who used to drive their old, heavy coups here on weekend nights before the price of a gallon of gas was comparable to a gallon of milk, which then came to the front door by the hands of a man and the wired crates he carried. And now Silvio.

The old man said, I haven't seen you for a couple of days.

I've been busy writing.

Writing?

Writing.

What have you been writing?

Stuff for the church.

What stuff?

Silvio leaned his back against the wall and slid down it until he was sitting next to the old man on the warm ground. His legs straightened and splayed before him on the concrete like a formless scarecrow. He said, Before someone can even be considered for sainthood they have to be nominated by a local congregation, so I'm going to need to get some support from the church. And then, farther down the line, the higher-ups will review my writings, among other things. I'm hoping they can publish it in the weekly bulletin and I can start to build a reputation.

A reputation?

Or a baseline, or a portfolio, or something. You know?

I don't.

Silvio shrugged and then reached down to brush off a fly that had landed on his outstretched and hairy shin. The old man continued,

Sil, I told you. This isn't what I was talking about. This saint stuff. It's crazy.

And I appreciate that you feel that way. But you need to understand that it's even crazier if I don't have your help. You've been here for a long time and if you vouch for me it could really help out.

I don't even know what I'm vouching for.

Just think of me like Saint Francis de Sales, only better.

Silvio. I don't know.

Silvio looked at him for another moment and offered a short smile before reaching his arm up awkwardly to give the old man's shoulder a soft squeeze. He rose to his feet and began walking up the hot pavement when the old man spoke again from behind him.

I'll see what I can do.

Silvio turned back toward the church with a grin and said, I appreciate it. I really do.

Silvio turned again to walk away, but threw his hands up and faced the old man. He said, But just so you know, I was kidding about that Saint Francis stuff. I'm not a great writer or anything like that.

It's okay.

I just wanted to be upfront with you.

I got it, Sil.

The old man offered a curt nod of his head as Silvio began to walk away again down the lonely sidewalk that, in two-point-one miles, would land him on his front doorstep.

Make lemonade, the old man called after him.

Silvio stopped. What?

I said make lemonade.

What on earth is that supposed to mean?

When life gives you lemons, make lemonade.

Where did that come from?

It's a saying.

Well why are you telling it to me?

I'm telling you to deal with what you got.

By making lemonade?

By making something bad into something good.

What's wrong with the lemons?

There's nothing wrong with the lemons.

You just said they were bad.

The lemons are fine. It's just that the lemonade is better.

Silvio raised a skeptical eyebrow. Just because you don't like lemons doesn't make that a saying.

My parents believed in small government, low tax rates, and an America that touted its diversity a hell of a lot more than it embodied it. They were proud Christians for one hour every Sunday, and I tried to be one too. But I didn't care much for the masses. Their numbing repetition of ritual never did it for me. It's a damn wonder why I ever got into the military with that kind of attitude, but that's exactly what I did. I figure you can look back on a lot of things in life that didn't turn out the way you wanted and not make much sense of them, even with all of that hindsight. I guess now I see that if only one or two decisions fit into that category, then that *can* be your whole life. Ask any non-habitual offender who is in prison. They'll tell ya. One or two decisions that don't jive with anything else you have ever done, and that can define every moment of your existence. Scary stuff.

Anyway, the people at the church were all friendly and they sucked on their smiles and I don't have much else to say about them. There was one Sunday, when I was a freshman in high school, and a boy from the congregation a few years older than me had just graduated and enlisted to be a marine. There were rumors in the school that he was gay, and he was teased for it, but he had never come out and nobody really knew. Anyway, the guy up front had just finished a short sermon on the irreligiousness of homosexuality when he had the soon-to-be marine stand and be the target of a large group prayer. While the rest of the congregation craned their bodies and bowed their necks to better pray for him, I couldn't help but wonder at if he was possibly gay, or not. I wondered what it was worth to pray for someone who is already doomed, because it seems like the waste of a perfectly good prayer. And here's the real justification behind the Don't Ask Don't Tell—not the wasted prayers, but the guilt. It's hard enough, if people are willing to face it, to live with the guilt of knowing that others are out there fighting and dying for their country while the average person, at most, contributes only a small wealth of taxes (and even those they complain about). And to complicate this guilt with the possibility that some soldiers are, by the civilian's measure, reprehensible beings, is too much for most people, as reprehensible as *they* are. Because they don't want to know about the lives of soldiers. They have standards for what type of person is good enough to die for them. Imagine that. But it's not that complicated in my mind. Not at all. If someone is willing to die for me then I'm just going to shut the fuck up about everything else. And if there's people who want to raise the standards in regards to who is qualified to die on their behalf, then it's my belief they should be the ones out there in the desert, sniffing out IED's so that the dogs and the rest of the decent folk can get on with being decent.

My friend Jude was like that. He was as decent as they came and willing to die for a lot of people who weren't worth it. But I'm biased in regards to Jude, who appeared on base without knowing a soul and actually *wanting* to go to war. By then, nobody in the unit had a mindset to make new friends, and Jude was met mostly by the unit as an outsider. But I tried not to be like that. I think it helped that I didn't know that Beatles song about his name. Some guys in the unit liked to serenade him with that song but I didn't figure out for a while what the hell was going on. Had these guys lost it or what? I thought they might be an on-base glee club that I didn't know about, but they weren't. They thought I was lying about not knowing the song, or that I was crazy. I wasn't either of those. And I don't know what the big deal is, because I still haven't ever heard the song they were singing.

Jude was the all-American type—tall, handsome, smart, and athletic. He was especially athletic. His limbs were long and tight, and even the most mundane task, such as brushing his teeth, was accompanied by the bulging and rippling of his forearm. He bounded through physical training exercises with ease, and even though I marveled at his and ability, from afar, for several weeks, it was he who first spoke to me. It was after hours, I was in my bunk, and he began a conversation about the book I was reading. It was a generic conversation about a generic fantasy paperback, and it didn't take much to figure out that he just needed to talk to somebody about anything. I didn't have much to say about myself, and so we talked about the book. I figured that the fantasy wouldn't interest him greatly, but that didn't stop me from filling him in on the important details of this particular installment (the fourth in the series), and about the significant bloodlines and mythic items that were the key players for the author. He listened intently and asked good questions, and while at first I thought he was just being polite, I began to sense his genuine interest. As our conversation moved forward, he claimed he hadn't read fantasy before. In school, he had occupied virtually allof his extracurricular hours with athletics, and when he was forced to read outside of his English syllabus, he gravitated toward paperback Westerns, because, in his words, they were easy and his father approved of them. I laughed at his logic and then agreed to put some Westerns on my to-read list, as long as he put some fantasy on his. He did, and our friendship started there.

What I already knew, and what Jude was soon to discover, is that reading is a great way to distract the mind. The closer we got to deploying, the more we emphasized spending every available minute with our noses in a book. As I drifted into numerous fantasy worlds, it became easier to not preoccupy my brain with all the bad things that could happen when we got to Iraq. The ideal soldier would keep his mind on the mission, and do a mental run through of how he or she was going to react in any given situation. That's how *they* stayed calm, and that's what made *them* good soldiers. I was *not* a good soldier, and so that kind of exercise simply scared the shit out of me. To think about all the different things that could go wrong made me freeze up. I'd get a weight on my chest and start gasping for air, and when I tried to calm myself down, the only activity my brain seemed willing to participate in was to catalogue every gruesome image from every war movie I'd ever seen. I could feel bullets distort the air around my head. I could hear their angry hiss. I could see thick streams of blood spouting from empty limbs. I could hear the scared voices of boys crying for their mothers. I could see bodies on the ground and the swaths of dust that took no hesitation in devouring the pools of warm blood.

Better to just read. Fantasy books. What isn't real can't hurt you, but it sure can distract you. That was my distraction of choice, and I wasn't the only one.

When the rest of the unit were playing video games and bragging about all the intercourse they had had with everyone else's mothers, Jude and I were swapping novels. They kidded us about being nerds, and we pointed out that they were playing video games and then we'd laugh. A nervous laugh, pre-war. I was glad that Jude had gotten into the fantasy—it made it easy to talk to him and acted as yet another distraction from the waiting hell. It also gave us something to bond over. It made us different. He liked the different structures and myths that made up each work—cosmology, economics, politics, religions, geography, technology, and so on—whereas I liked the magic and the dragons. Mostly the dragons. There'd be some sword fighting and some romance and some betrayal and I'd be reading it like, Where are all the fucking dragons at?

Jude laughed and said I had to think about more than just the dragons, but whatever. It felt good to have somebody there.

On the eve that we arrived in Iraq, I came across a character in my fantasy novel that was a soldier—a good one. She'd seen a lot of war and so she'd seen a lot of death. Swords and shields and all of that. She was focused and calm in her duty, like I should have been. This woman was captured by the bad guys (heaven forbid) and they were throwing all these politics at her about what she could do to save her life—what they wanted her to tell them—but this character didn't care. She was stone cold. She laughs in the face of his captors and says, You think that I think of my life as some kind of precious thing?

She said that right to their face. It wasn't a bluff either, I tell you. This girl was as genuine as any fake character could be, and all I could think about was the heaviness of the question she posed. I wondered how much death can one person see before they can no longer value the gift of life. And can someone even know when they get to that point? I guess that's what really gets me—the possibility of something once precious being cast into the wind without a thread of recognition or regret. If something like life can lose its value then nothing is sacred.

Then again, it's easy for a character that's not real—that has no life—to cast such a gift out. After all, she is just a bunch of words. And her words are just the words of more words. Can that be precious?

That character made me realize something though. I never aspired to being any kind of war hero or five-star general. I planned on spending the breadth of my military career as close to the bottom rungs as I could. I'd rather have my life in someone else's hands than anyone's life in mine. When the warm blood of fellow soldiers started to run into the sandy streets, I wanted it to stay on those streets and not on my hands. It takes someone special to order men to death. A real conviction that I never possessed. And it doesn't matter if I trusted those people or not. My life was going to be threatened, and when the time came I was going to do all I could to preserve it, simple as that. It didn't matter to me whose hands my blood ends up on, so long as there is none on mine. I don't know if that worked out for me though, keeping the blood off, because when Jude died over there in that hell hole, it did a number on me.

Paths for the Blind

It was dark, and under a starred night sky walked Silvio in the manner of a man more insane than he is—hands deep in his pockets and neck flopped back so as to appreciate the sky above while maintaining his wobbly, sickening gait. Where he saw only minor fragments of light were gas giants, and between those, in the cavernous black dark, hid the cosmic dust of entire galaxies that swirled and blossomed in a way that only gravity could manage. As he looked into the resonant ink, he couldn't help but wonder at the worlds it held, and his own longing for them. But for what good was his longing? What good was he? If he were to journey to some far-off, wondrous planet, what could the individual saint offer there? Of all of Earth's marvels—staples in his life—he could reproduce none of them. On those distant surfaces, he could expound for days on the qualities of the automobile, and the airplane, and the firearm, and how doctors could perform surgeries with utensils that worked at a microscopic level, and when the planet's natives asked him to duplicate any of it, he could not. And if they gave him everything he needed, how long then? Could he create a refrigerator if he gave his life to the task? A telephone? Certainly not a microwave. So what was he without the all of human achievement at his back? The best he could hope for was to create a piece of art that encompassed the empty struggling of his humanity and hope that their species could relate. They too must appreciate the unnerving size of it all. They too must carry around with them the questions that have no answers. Always carrying them, everywhere. And him, just a scared rocketeer who hauls tired human relics that process food and process words and compress air and play music and track time and capture photographs—all on the verge of extinction within his incapable hands. He'd try to tell them how many years and lives were given to the development of each product, except that he himself didn't know, and so he would tell them nothing.

He paused in his walk and blinked hard, because even if he summoned an astronaut's bravery, he first had to choose a point of light that they'd assure him was a planet. Out there, where there were as many stars as grains of sand in a desert, or some other incomprehensible amount that meant a vastness beyond his or any person's grasp. And no amount of lenses could see to infinity and did he even want to know what waited beyond *that* weighty nothing?

He reached the entrance of the church and gave one last look at the sky before going inside and putting its high roof between him and it all. Inside, on the far side of the nave, Silvio could hear rummaging in the back room. He walked on light feet through the pews and found the old man dusting around the church's gold tabernacle. Silvio leaned in the open doorway and cleared his throat loudly, but the old man held up a single finger to suggest that he needed a little more time. The small tabernacle's doors were open, and the old man navigated around its interior with a white, linen rag. He said that even God's apparatus is susceptible to dust. Next to the tabernacle were a pair of beautiful chalices with sterling cups and a matching, gold-plated dish. The old man picked up a small spray bottle from next to his feet, gave the rag two spurts, and then set about polishing each piece of the ornate silverware. Silvio grew bored watching him and wandered back into the muted nave. He patrolled up and down the pew aisles running his finger along their narrow backs and eventually took a seat in the back row. Several minutes later the old man appeared from the back room and he too moved between the pews with his large, dusty rag which he ran delicately over the smooth and lacquered wood of the pews. Silvio watched him. Then he said, You ever just look up at the stars and wonder about it?

The old man pressed the white cloth over the dark wood of the final row's leg support and he said, I like looking at the stars as much as the next person.

Is that a lot?

I suppose not.

They were the only two in the church's dim lighting. The old man took a seat on shaky knees next to Silvio, where the reflection of the room's soft light made his skin look waxen and bloodless. Smoky light bulbs and ceiling fans spun slowly enough to question whether they actually moved air and thus question their very purpose. The stained glass windows lost their brilliance in the night, each pane adopting a dark purple hue that appeared so from inside and out. The dark pit of the carpet reflected the soft tremble of candle light—the white wax sticks, their brass caps, and the tiny fire that burned eternal yet never appeared to move down each slow fuse as if the church had devised the recipe for clean and perpetual energy.

The old man said, Still writing?

Yes. I'm trying, anyway.

I'll bet that it's hard.

You'd win that bet.

I never could write. English was always my least favorite subject. More of a numbers guy, myself.

I don't remember having any talent for it either, said Silvio. And I could never get over the idea that so many writers went to their grave thinking that they weren't any good at it.

Any good at going to their grave?

Any good at writing.

Oh. Yeah. That just sounds like a typical writer problem.

I just mean that it's remarkable to spend your life feeling like you just aren't very good at what you do. Or, if not that, then you die knowing that you were never appreciated. I couldn't imagine being at the end of my life and thinking that maybe I'd wasted it. Writers like Melville and Dickinson and Poe and Hurston. That's a hard way to die. And then, however many years later, to have people begin to recognize and appreciate your work? After you're dead? That's sick.

The old man shook his head and said, I guess that's just not a worry that I can relate to.

Silvio stole a glance at the portrait of the old man's wrinkled features. He said, Are you afraid of being forgotten?

The old man replied, People can't forget what they never knew.

Does that bother you?

The old man shook his head again. No, he said. I don't think so. I never had aspirations to get remembered by anybody. I've always just tried to do right for the people that I care about. Are you going to forget about me when I'm gone?

Of course not.

The old man offered a smile of great satisfaction. He said, Well there ya have it.

Silvio partially rolled his eyes and then focused his attention on the fan directly above them that, by his estimation, must be broken to be spinning so slowly.

I guess you're right, Silvio said. Maybe you should be the one writing.

We already decided that I'm not any good at that kind of stuff. Why don't we try to figure you out? Maybe just tell me about your approach.

I don't have one. I just try to create good writing.

And what is good writing?

Good writing marries Truth and Beauty.

That's lovely, the old man said.

That's because I didn't write it.

Well it's a nice place to start.

Silvio shook his head in frustration and said, The problem is that I know no Truths. And if I did, I certainly don't know how to make them beautiful.

The old man frailly leaned forward and ran the rag across the bottom of his seat and then inspected the white cloth as if its dusty sediment held secrets of great import. Look around you, Silvio. This place isn't for people who know Truth. This place is for the people who are, at least, willing to look for it.

I guess that I'm still looking.

We all are.

Does anyone ever find it?

If they want to? All the time.

How?

The old man placed the bespeckled rag on his lap and reached into a wooden bracket attached to the pew ahead of them. Every church pew had this same cubby, and from it the old man pulled a worn copy of the Bible. He flipped his wrist up. Right here, he said.

The main door of the church opened behind them and the two turned in their pew to see an older lady peek her head inside. They both waved and their waves were friendly enough to suggest familiarity, and she edged her shoulder inside enough to give a wave back and she reminded the old man that he was the one locking up tonight. He said that he always was, and she wished them a good night before slipping back into the darkness.

They both turned in the pew to face the front of the church again. The old man said, Son, you've been telling me about this idea of yours about being a saint, and if you're trying to be a Christian saint then there *is* one truth. It's right here.

The old man tapped the Bible that he then placed on the pew next to him.

Silvio chewed on the inside of his lip. He said, I know that. But maybe the omniscient, omnipresent—you know, the omni words—can't be understood in that way. I'm not convinced that one collection of testimonies can possibly embody the everything that ever has been and will be, everywhere. How can the alpha and the omega be compressed into one book? It should be more complex than that.

Son, those aren't just testimonies. That's the word of God in there, as spoken through his prophets and the like.

Prophets declaring themselves prophets doesn't make them anything. Just arrogant, and big mouthed. Claiming to be a hero or a villain can't alter your very essence into something it is not—into something it is not designed to be. I've met people that had no claim for what they thought they were, and the ones that did hardly ever got it right by my estimation.

The old man ran a hand over his sparsely haired head. He said, Well if we are going by that logic, I'd declare you to be something like a Quaker.

I'm not a Quaker, Silvio said.

Okay, but that goes to your point.

What point?

The old man said, That, when confronted with a mirror, we hardly recognize ourselves. That, if we take someone at their word, they will likely fool us. But they are what they are, and you're no different Silvio. I know that I, for one, am comforted by the fact that inside all of us is the true knowledge that something, somewhere, knows what we really are, and a time will come when we will need to answer for whatever that is.

Well if we are what we are, then what is there to answer for?

The old man's beaten face didn't change and neither did his tone. His right hand still rested on the worn Bible cover as he stared forward at the generic jacket of the hymn books shelved in the pew's cubby.

It's not a test where everyone gets the same questions. We each of us have our own events to answer for, and the better we answer for them here the better we can answer for them wherever we are going. We know what we are supposed to do, but whether we do it or not is something else entirely. Whether we do it or not is what we must answer for.

Now the old man leaned forward on the pew with his hands folded in his lap and his feet gone under the bench like some existential gargoyle. Silvio measured him momentarily with a look of concern and then diverted his attention toward the front of the nave again. On the wall hung a large crucifix with an exhausted depiction of Jesus carved skillfully out of the wood's origin. Like the pews, it was heavily lacquered, and it glowed dully in response to the church's indistinct lighting. Even with the poor lighting he could make out the defeated features immortalized by the carving. An alleged god come to the dirty stratum of man to share a message of life and love and here hung the response to such things. And what else to do with a slain god other than forge trophies of its defeat?

Through his stony lips the old man said, If you were to send a blind man down some path, would you let him know where that path ended up if you knew so yourself?

What path?

Any path. Would you tell him?

Well I guess if it ended up nice I'd go ahead and tell him. If it didn't end up nice I'd as soon not send him down the path in the first place.

And if you didn't know how the path ended up?

Silvio considered this for a minute.

If I didn't know how it ended up then there wouldn't be much to offer as far as him taking down that path or not. I'd tell him to go right ahead. As far as some blind man is concerned that path is as good as any other.

What if it ends up bad?

Well, there's no telling what worse or better path he would have taken. If it ends up bad there's no telling that down another path it wouldn't have ended up worse. If you ask me, a blind man knows more about bad luck than just about anybody. They don't seem like the bunch to bemoan a little misstep here or there.

The old man laughed and said, No, they don't.

What are you asking me about this anyway? You got a blind man in your life that needs directions?

The old man was still hunched forward in the pew. It's a parable, he said.

A parable about what?

He said, It just depends on who you think is blind and who you think isn't.

I worked through high school at a local grocery store. I was technically hired as a bagger, but I had to do a little bit of everything—bag groceries and stock shelves and sweep aisles, and so on. Basically anything that limited me and my fellow bagger's contact with the customers, which is fair because this kid Peter had the same gig as me but he mostly was just stoned out of his mind the whole time he was on the clock. He'd light up in the parking lot in his car before his shift, and he'd go back out there on every break. He smelled like mother nature and did every part of the job with an idiot's smile on his face—always reeking of cheap weed. I think he got the job due to some distant family relation calling in a favor. But honestly, aside from his habit of snacking on the store's fresh produce, he was a pretty good worker, so long as customers couldn't smell him and didn't look into his eyes long enough to appreciate just how bloodshot they were. Drugs never appealed to me, but eight hours of bagging peanut butter and toilet paper and yogurt and eggs and shampoo and fruit snacks and bread and milk can almost drive a man to smoke anything. After a particularly depressing shift I took up Peter's offer to go to his car. I had no point of reference in terms of how high I was, but he offered up a string of muffled giggles and kept telling me, You're baked out of your gourd, man. He continued laughing and said that people in there were going to confuse me with one of the cakes in the bakery section. What kind of cake bags groceries? I didn't know, but I laughed too. When we got back to work it felt like the whole world had gotten itself a coat of molasses. I suspect it took me about thirty minutes to load one bag of canned corn and tomato soup. After a few customers I was approached by my manager and was sure that I was in trouble. I was, but not the kind that I thought. She told me that there had been an accident and I was needed in our produce section. I arrived in produce to find a cart of cleaning supplies waiting for me, as well as a trail of diarrhea leading to the restrooms. Apparently, somebody had shit their pants while looking for some properly ripe bananas. That was maybe the worst thirty minutes of my life up to that point, and though it had nothing to do with the weed, I never smoked pot again. To this day, any time that I smell weed, it comes strongly associated with the smell of that foul diarrhea.

When we met later, I gathered from Jude that about the same time I was putting my time in at the grocery store, he was spending summers working on his family's ranch. I really envied that part of his history—being one with the land, out in the sun. Even now I can see him in my mind's eye tilling in the dirt, or doing whatever it is people do on ranches. He'd take his shirt off to better soak the sun's rays into his body. He'd wear a baseball cap because he always wore a baseball cap. Shirt off, cap on, working in the sun. I can envision his strong, tanned arms with their muscles bulging from underneath. Worn out blue jeans and a proper pair of work boots, doing ranch things.

That was one of the only jobs he and I ever had before we signed up for Uncle Sam and swapped the grocery store and the ranch for a military base. In my early days of enlistment I'd spend a lot of my spare time around the base at the armory, usually just to shoot hoops. Long before I got there though, someone decided it would be a good idea to make up the dullness of the armory with the strategic placement of historical artifacts. War things. Black and white photos of past battalions and dual-tip fighter planes. A piece of shrapnel from this battle, and an old landmine from that one. They displayed an old artillery round about the size of my torso.

I didn't pay attention to much of anything in school, and I figure now that mingling around the armory must have been my first lesson in History. Part museum, part graveyard—a place to hold Mass for all things unholy and God-forsaken. It's the kind of Mass that will really make you believe in things too. Like, some of the men who mugged me from those black and white photos must have been about as brave as you could make them. How else could you enter into a battlefield where the bullets are as big as the soldiers? Soldiers used to entrench themselves a few hundred yards apart while the other side would roll down great clouds of mustard gas at them and pray that the wind didn't change directions. And the gas would blister the hell out of whatever it came into contact with—skin, nasal passages, airways, lungs, you name it.

As I continued to hover over the photographs and captions, I was approached by a second lieutenant who playfully slapped at the basketball that I had pinned under my arm. He gave a thoughtful look to the photos that I was studying and nodded his head in understanding and approval. He said, That mustard gas was some real nasty shit. And it was never supposed to kill anybody, not right away anyway. Did you know that? No? The German's were more devious than that. Ideally, the gas would inflict enough damage to take a soldier out of battle, but not so much damage that it would kill him. You see? That way, not only would the allies be down a soldier, but they would also have to use valuable resources and space to try to keep the inflicted soldiers alive. Infirmaries would be flooded with casualties and the trenches were filled with terrified souls, wondering when the next gas would come. It was brilliant warfare. Psychological. Brutal.

He shook his head grimly as if to acknowledge the aforementioned brutality, and we bowed our heads in an informal moment of silence. He gave me a parting pat on the arm and continued down one of the armory's halls to his office. He surely didn't think about it, but, had I been in uniform, the place on my arm where he patted me would display one meager chevron. The symbol of my standing in this army. The definitive proof that, had I been an enlisted man in 1917, I would be the one eating the gas. I would be the one that the enemy wanted to push as agonizingly close to death as possible without actually dying. I would be the one huddled in the wet trenches, waiting for the toll of the bell that warned of an incoming chemical gas attack—waiting for the sulfurous mist to settle in and blister every inch of me, inside and out.

Sadly enough, my rudimentary lesson on early chemical warfare wasn't what stood out to me most during my tour through the armory. Nope. The thing that haunts me most from that day is the pictures and captions of the World War One trench knife. This thing looked like a fucking ice pick with a brass knuckle grip, but it is the three sides to the blade that will really get you. Now, if someone were to stab you with a knife, the wound would have a level of symmetry to it—a two-sidedness, if you will. A wound like this is relatively easy to stitch and to heal, but adding a third side to the blade complicates the nature of the inflicting wound. It makes it nearly impossible for the wound to clot, and much harder for it to be stitched. If someone gets pricked by one of these blades, they are going to be in a world of hurt. Even if they do manage to survive until the help arrives, that third side creates such a mess that there's not a lot to be done anyway.

It's a real rotten utensil, and so you know what happened to it? Some people organized some conventions, and at these conventions they decided to banish weapons like this tri-blade from the battlefield. Imagine that— deciding that a particular weapon is simply *too much* weapon for combat. I've said that I'm no wise guy when it comes to history, but I figure this must be some kind of head scratcher to anyone.

I simply don't understand those rules. Apparently you can stab a man without wanting to kill him. If that's the case, then I'd just as rather not stab the man at all. And if I did? Well then I suppose I'd want him dead. It's no good for him to go off and get healed up and come back to do some stabbing of his own. And when he does come back, what's keeping him from packing a three bladed treat for me? Is he not going to do that because some conventions held 100 years ago suggested that he shouldn't? I doubt it. And I certainly aint willing to bet my life on it. He probably thinks Geneva is a brand of shampoo and Hague is a type of sandwich bun. I can only imagine him, or myself, getting in trouble for using a weapon like that—getting in trouble for killing a man, during war, with an unapproved method. Someone will have to explain to me what History makes of that.

The blade I saw in the armory on that day haunted me more than any other artifact before or since. It marked upon me a wound of doubt not easily healed or stitched up. It would be some time before I managed my way out of military duty, but some part of me checked out the day I saw the trench knife. Some part of me was done when I saw the madness in that armory—a decent and regulated mode of annihilation.

Silvio Submission One:

There was a young man who was born into tragedy, and agriculture. For seven generations the Woodlief family had been plagued—not by drought or hail—but by lightning. They were struck in garden tractors and row crop tractors. They were struck when the cab was open and when it was closed. The first generation Woodlief patriarch was fifty-seven years old when his iron spade was struck mid-swing without so much as a cloud in the sky. Twelve years later his son's push plow was hit, killing him instantly. When they finally found the horse that was pulling the plow, its tail was naught but a singed nub of hair. The young man's great-great-great-grandfather was smote on his porch while drinking his morning coffee out of a tin mug. The following spring his great-great grandfather was just a young boy climbing a tree when the tree was hit, splitting it nearly in half. He survived that strike, but wasn't so lucky when, twenty-one years later, he was killed by lightning as he lay irrigation pipe in a light rain storm.

By the time the young man became a young man he was the last of the Woodlief patriarchy. If a cloud in the sky had the slightest shade of gray, he could only be found cowered underneath the dining room table, where his hands covered his ears and he shivered. The fear alone was almost enough to kill him. In his mind's eye he could see the lurking bolts ricochet from cloud to cloud, discharging and recoiling, just waiting for the opportunity to burn him into the earth. To return him to the dust from whence he came.

When thunderheads got close enough to speak to him, he groveled from below the table like a dog on the fourth of July. And when those flares from the lightning were within sight of the house, it burned onto his retinas the fallen faces of his ancestry. The only Woodlief family tree that mattered consisted of a forked bolt of lightning, and where that bolt met the soil of the earth was the gaunt portrait of our young man.

In his heart he knew that should God really want him dead, there were countless ways for him to do it, but this didn't keep him from spending years of his adolescence hiding under the table. As he came into his early twenties he decided that his own cowardice was an affront to God's order and to himself—if lightning would not strike at his ghastly figure from there, it was not because God was merciful toward him. His life was no life to live. His sisters encouraged him to stay under the table until he could reinvigorate the family name, but he refused to take any agency from the divine. If God wanted to end the line, then end the line he would. God was God, and our young man was still only a young man.

And so, the next time a thundercloud cleared its throat and the brilliant spider webs of electricity moved into the acres of the farm, he could be found in the middle of a field—a metal pipe fixed to his back like the sashimono of feudal samurai. He stood there that night, unharmed, until the sky went back to sleep, and then so did he.

To do something once can be the effect of temptation, but by this ritual he no longer envisioned himself tempting fate, but embracing it. The next storm that came through, and the dozen after that, were all met by the young man and his metal rod. His sisters begged him to stop mocking the sky—to stop tempting the tragedy that ran like iron through the blood in their veins. But he didn't listen. Surely if God didn't want him to be struck by lightning, then he wouldn't be struck. Each time he marched onto the field under a shaded sky, he didn't do so as a heretic, and he didn't do so with fear or defiance—only with the certainty that the outcome was exactly as it should be.

He and his sashimono survived thirteen storms with that attitude. Thirteen. On the morning after the fourteenth his sisters found his torched, crumpled body. Seared onto his shirt was the exact shape of the bolt as it coursed through his figure, and onto his face the countenance of a perplexed buffoon.

The Parade

The parade sailed by Silvio's gaze like the old reel film of some incoherent circus. There were horses, and llamas, and dogs, and humans, and they were all dressed in rampant colors of no theme or reason. There were cowboys, and athletes, and boosters, and nobodies, and they marched proudly like as many fascists. Amidst the mobilized army of people and creatures came fire trucks from a number of decades as if a time machine sat at the entrance of Main Street and hailed them through one at a time in order to give the masses a history lesson in the spectacle of old men riding old vehicles. Next came a similar exhibition of tractors for spectators to marvel at their size and guess at their purpose. When the local beauty queen passed by perched atop a red Ford Thunderbird, she waved out at the ogling of the men, the scrutiny of the women, and the empty watch of Silvio. Children swarmed the sidewalks and the streets like a pack of wild dogs and they flaunted their swelling candy bags to peers and parents alike. Silvio stooped to pick up the occasional hard candy that landed near his feet and poked through a handful of it before he selected one and tucked the rest of the noisy wrappers into his short's pocket. Smiling cowgirls clopped by on top of bannered horses, and the kids with all the candy laughed guiltily when the horse dung splattered thick and green upon the asphalt. There were generic sedans that crept along with nothing more than the decal of a local business plastered to their doors, and there were big trucks that pulled big, slatted trailers that were filled up by the high school's sports teams. The volleyball players wore spandex bottoms and the football players wore their helmets and they both fit in among the horse dung and the fire trucks just as well as the rest of it. Last was the remnant of the school's marching band, with the droll blare of their brass horns unable to match, in volume or vigor, the pop hits that blasted from the regional radio station's trailer two floats ahead. When the last of them had gone, Silvio was finally able to cross the street, dodging the splayed patches of excrement, and walk on to the church several blocks away. He took a spot next to the old man on the front steps, where he apologized for being late.

Silvio said, So what did you think?

About the writing?

Yeah about the writing. Are they going to put it in the bulletin?

There is no They, Silvio. It's just Mrs. Crawford, and she said she didn't get it. She thought it was a little too grim for the bulletin.

Silvio flashed a look of confusion. Too grim? I didn't mean it to be grim.

I know you didn't. But you have to think about your audience—about the congregation. They don't care to read your musings on God striking down some poor farm boy.

I never said that God struck him down.

Sil, I just think that you should tone it down a little bit. If I were you, I would just have less death and destruction next time.

No you wouldn't.

What?

Well if you were me then that isn't what you would be doing. If you were me then you'd just be me. You would be doing what I'm doing, because that's what me does.

The old man shook his head. He said, I just mean that if I were in your position, that's what I would do. I would tone it down.

Okay.

The streets around the church temporarily populated with parade attendants making their way home. Parents walked with shed jackets and fold out chairs tucked under their arms, while grandparents shuffled along with the small and measured gait signature to their elderly demographic. Children skipped on their sugar highs and the slow tinder of barbequed meats began to fill the air around the old man and Silvio. In a distant backyard came the violent startup and concussive pumping of a lawnmower engine. The sun was prominent, but not hot, and the occasional soothing breeze had passerby's commenting on what a perfect spring day it was.

The good news is that Mrs. Crawford said that she liked your style, and that no one has ever submitted any writing like that before. You should go talk to her. She seemed to be excited that someone was taking an interest in the bulletin.

She did?

Indeed. She told me to get you to submit something else—something a little less gloomy.

I can do that.

I'm sure you can. But Silvio, listen: I promised you I would support you on whatever this pursuit of yours is, but I also have the responsibility to urge you to do something a little more practical.

It's been noted.

The old man offered a sarcastic thanks before Silvio rose from the steps.

Silvio said, I didn't see you at the parade this morning.

That's because I wasn't there.

Why not?

Because I don't like parades.

Within a military unit you get a lot of different backgrounds, and these backgrounds lead to a type of necessary small talk. Mostly guys bragged on the girls they had hooked up with in the past, or told raunchy stories from their high school years—tales of hacking the school district's security firewall, planting trees on the football field's fifty-yard-line, pooping in file cabinets, and drawing cartoon penii on anything with a surface. But it wasn't all adolescent gab and posturing, because guys shared dreams too—what they aspired to, what they wanted out of the military, and what they wanted out of life. Sergeant Murphy said it was his dream to visit every national monument and national park in the United States, and when he had done that he wanted to go worldwide with his visits—his ultimate goal was to see a mountain gorilla in Africa's Congo. He was just beginning to go into detail about the stuff that he had already seen when Private Church interrupted and asked Murphy if he had been to Mount Rushmore. Murphy hadn't, and Church, scoffing, said that he was wasting his time seeing anything else. Church claimed that Mount Rushmore was the single most impressive monument on the planet. This statement was met by a spat of laughter and the following statements from some of the guys:

Is this your first time outside of South Dakota?

Dude, have you heard of the Great Pyramids?

China has this wall that they've built, and I've heard it's pretty impressive.

Church dismissed the sarcasm with a wave of his hand and patiently waited out all of the laughter and eye rolling. He then referred to the Pyramids and the Great Wall as crumbling exercises in amateur architecture— that they're the kinds of things kids create with building bricks. But the great stone faces of Mount Rushmore? He argued that humans would be extinct for thousands of years, all manner of infrastructure would have long melted back into the earth, and the faces of those men would still be plastered on the side of that mountain. By the time the gorillas in the Congo had evolved themselves into higher thinking beasts, they'd eventually stumble upon Rushmore, and whatever god they had worshipped up to that point would either be erased, or would have its visual manifestation.

Jesus Christ, he said. People get all worked up over the likes of Easter Island and Stonehenge and all that crap—could you imagine some Neanderthal coming out of a forest clearing and seeing that shit carved into the side of a mountain? Those men are gods for a long time to come.

He pointed his finger at Murphy and nodded his head at something none of us understood. He said, Mount Rushmore my friend. That's where you need to go.

And that's how it went most of the time—a lot of bullshit to fill up the time. And some of that bullshit involved guys explaining how Uncle Sam ended up calling the shots, and though each person's story has its own unique details, it wasn't difficult for me to trace dominant themes among my peers. Here's how I figure it: there's three different motivation types for joining the service. The first type is guys like me. We're the guys that joined up because the military offered opportunities we weren't going to get anywhere else. Growing up, I was a normal enough kid. I played on the football team, but I wasn't good. In a small town like mine, if you were able to walk and chew bubble gum at the same time then there was a varsity spot lined up for you. The same thing went for my academics—I passed my classes but I wasn't on the track to win a Nobel Prize. I might have been able to cut it in college, but nobody in my family had ever went and I'm not the pioneering type. It was my idea to graduate high school, find a decent, bottom-tier job and, in time, work my way up to a position that made a half-decent buck. So when I was a senior in high school and we had some Army recruiters come to the school during a job fair, I initially went to their table because I needed to prove to my guidance counselor that I had visited at least five tables. My whole perception of the military was steeped in action films and World War Two dramas, and so I couldn't imagine a place for myself within its system. But the guy sitting at the table was real charismatic and he got to talking to me about what the military was really about. And really, it is a goldmine of opportunity. He mapped out all the different paths available to me as I advanced in my career. He explained to me the opportunities I'd have with going to college, officer school, flight school, and so on. It seemed like the best thing to do, for me. I could be a mechanic, or a I could be a general. On top of all of that, I was also paid to stay in good physical health, and I would have opportunities to travel the world. And fine . . . so maybe being stationed in a foreign country as an occupying military force doesn't exactly qualify, in the traditional sense, as "traveling" or "seeing the world," but it does offer a view that I couldn't get from my own neighborhood. The recruiter wasn't lying about that.

But, the fact is, I was seventeen years old at the time and I got caught up in something that I didn't understand. Making the decision to be active duty in the military isn't exactly like deciding on which college to attend—you can't approach your commanding officer mid-semester and ask to switch to the major where you don't get shot at. And I wasn't the only one with doubts. Maybe the other guys in the unit wouldn't admit it openly, but I could see it in some of their eyes. It's difficult to keep a poker face when you're constantly thinking, "what the fuck did I get myself into?" Part of me was glad to know that I wasn't the only one to make this mistake, and that little observation gave me some comfort in regard to my own stupidity, but when I realized that these were the very guys that I would rely on to save my life, I became nauseous.

Sometimes we'd go off base disguised in civilian clothing, but when a dozen guys with the same buzz-cut are sitting at the same table in the same restaurant, it was crystal clear who and what we were. Now, I was proud to be a serviceman, but I was always uncomfortable when civilians would come up and let me know how proud they were of me. I was even more uncomfortable when the people would express their pride after I had consumed enough alcohol to kill a small mule. They didn't seem to be bothered by my glassy eyes and stupid grin as they'd thank me for my service and thank me for protecting their freedoms and tell me how brave I was and make sure I knew I had their full support. I guess it was a nice thing for them to do, but I sure didn't sign up for any of those people. They didn't so much as cross my mind. I didn't think once of defending freedoms or branding the world with an American flag, or getting shot at. I was an opportunist—I thought of it as a job—and so I didn't care for people treating me like I was a hero when I felt like anything but. Loggers and fishermen were more likely to die in their line of work than I was in mine, and yet I've never heard anybody thank a logger for his or her service.

The second type of motivation for enlistment is what I call the John Rambo effect. This theme is self-explanatory—these guys had seen the Rambo films a few too many times. And I don't call it this because of the super soldier, rabid individual accomplishments of these servicemen, but because of their burning desire to blow shit up. These guys love blowing shit up, and the military offered them an appropriate, if not glorified, outlet to do so. These guys are great to have around at times—they'd whoop and holler and give high fives whenever we got out on the range. And when they weren't on the range, they would whoop and holler at their video games as they blew shit up on there too. They would continually grunt their satisfaction at the weapons and instruments of war around us. They'd snap pictures with their shirts off, sunglasses on, and assault rifles shooting from the hip like you see on movie posters. I've seen the Rambo's get the same praise from civilians that I was so uncomfortable with. They were always very cordial and accommodating to the admiring civilians. I imagine I could always tell what they were thinking when civilians would come up and tell them how much they admired their sacrifices—the Rambo's would smile and nod, *I don't know what this person is talking about because I'm just here to blow shit up.*

The last type of motivation is for the idealistic folk. The Henry David Thoreau's of the world. The Jude motive. Soldiers like Jude joined up because they wanted to join in the battle against evil. They envisioned an America that's always under attack and always being plotted against, and they saw it as their duty to protect it. These guys love America like I wish I could love *anything*. For them, any country that wasn't America sure as hell wanted to be, and it was their duty to help those countries along on their democratic path. Heroes of these soldiers include: Babe Ruth, Toby Keith, Ronald Reagan, Jesus Christ, and Superman. These soldiers don't just believe in *things*, they believe in America. I envied these men and I tried to be infected by their idealism, but it's not something that is easily transferable. Maybe more time with Jude would have touched me with his attitude, maybe not.

And as if my mind wasn't fragile enough following 9/11, it did me no favor to suddenly realize that even these guys—the Teddy Roosevelt's of the unit—had their doubts. Maybe not in regard to the war, but at least in their responsibility to it. For Jude, it was his wife. It seemed to me to almost be a slip of thought when he first mentioned his marriage. He wore no ring and when I surprisedly mentioned that I didn't know he was married, he tried to pretend like he hadn't heard me and then attempted to change the conversation. I didn't catch on to this in the moment, and so I daftly pressed on about his apparent secret. Jude tried to play it cool, but I had no trouble recognizing that all too familiar "what the fuck did I get myself into?" look that came onto his face. The only thing that he would concede to me is how she fought tooth and nail to keep him from enlisting. And why wouldn't she? It must be an uncomfortable sensation to have your husband choose his love for country over his love for you. He left behind love and life to go to war, which must be impossible for just about anyone to understand. I thought that she obviously didn't understand the man that she loved and married—at least not like I did. Of course Jude was going to enlist after 9/11—America was under attack and it needed its Jude's to protect it. (In Jude's own words) How could he live with himself if he sat by idly as terrorists attacked freedom, God, and his family's peace of mind? He said that he thought he was doing it for her but then shook his head absently and just muttered the words "I don't know" to himself. He must have carried a lot on his shoulders. More than I can imagine. I know that it tore him up to have to leave his wife, but he believed in America—and I've already covered what's at stake when real believing is involved.

So we trained. We kept in shape and honed our skills and when we got the occasional leave from base, we all looked the same. When people thanked me, they should have been thanking the likes of Jude, but I guess that in the eyes of most civilians we were all the same. Just a bunch of buzz cuts. I wanted to tell them that I'm not the kind of soldier that they were thinking of. I wasn't for king or for country. I wasn't for God or for family. I was confused and I was recruited for the world's greatest military power at a fucking job fair held in the gymnasium of my old high school. I'm a soldier, but I don't got soul. I just needed to visit five different tables to get a pass from my guidance counselor. Five different tables. If I didn't visit the table of the United States Army I probably would have opted for the information technologies table. Maybe technical school. I got soul, but I'm not a soldier. Except I am a soldier. I'm a soldier and I'm getting deployed and I'm in trouble.

Silvio Submission Two:

WATER CYCLE

I recall the diagrams
shown by the grade-school teacher—
the sun with the sunglasses,
the wide-eyed rain in frozen freefall,
clouds puffed with the exertion of blowing.

The mountains were like toll booths,
the burdened clouds emptying
their pockets of rain to advance
thinly to the empty deserts beyond.

But after all the personification
and the directional arrows cut
from construction paper, I only
wonder now if the light nimbus cloud

overhead could once have been part
of the Jordan River, or if the ocean I
step out of may one day rain upon the
heads of my unborn children.

Expectations, Silence

T he only building in the entire town that stood higher than two stories was the county's lone hospital, which was every bit of three
stories. Silvio routinely walked through its parking lot because it lay
between his house and a large field next to the town's largest trailer park,
where he had recently adopted an abandoned shed that he used to feed the
area's stray cats. It was common for bedbound patients of the hospital to
look idly out their windows and ask nurses about the young man lugging
large bags of cat food. Nurses often responded to these patients with the enduring advice that the patient should get more rest. During his mornings at
the shed, Silvio spotted what he counted to be a dozen unique cats, though,
given his inability to decipher some of them that looked alike, he figured it
to be anywhere upwards of seventeen. They went through a sixteen-pound
bag of dry food every two days and he had already cleared an area within
the decrepit space to place a space heater for the fall and winter chill.

The small buildings downtown were home to small business owners,
with the exception of banks and insurance companies, which all carried
national brands. At the turn of the century there were a total of four gas
stations, but only one of them remained after a national chain moved into
town, opened a truck stop, and started selling gas at ninety-nine cents a
gallon as a grand opening promotion. The promotion went on for fifty-
four days, which is exactly how long its corporate strategists calculated they
needed to monopolize gas sales and do irrevocable damage to the outdated
and inferior stations. It worked. What was left was a 24/7 monstrosity of
a truck stop that churned out fuel, fried food, and sixty-four ounce soft
drinks in equal measure. When it rained, all the excess water grabbed the
oils on the ground, which sat atop the flowing water like diluted water colors, and washed them away into the truck stop's large grated gutter that it

placed on the property border to its neighboring business—a small diner that looked to blow over at the mere shudder of passing semi-trucks.

The diner's interior matched its dated exterior. Inside, Silvio ran his hand over the decades old wallpaper appreciatively as he exited the bathroom and headed back to his booth where the old man was waiting for him. In front of Silvio was a full breakfast plate of bacon and eggs and pancakes, and in front of the old man was a cup of coffee. The old man stirred his drink absently while looking at the rain running down the large glass panes while Silvio ate. When he paused from eating long enough to notice the old man's gaze, he too glanced out at the falling rain.

I applied to have a foreign exchange student live with me for a semester.

You did?

Silvio nodded while he ran a napkin over his mouth, inspected the napkin, and ran it over his mouth again. He brushed errant food particles off his pant legs and said, Yeah. I thought it was a good opportunity to mentor anyone brave enough to want to live here for a few months. My application was turned down though. They said I wasn't exactly what they were looking for when it came to being a host family.

I don't imagine you are.

Silvio motioned with his chin toward the cup in front of the old man and said, Is that coffee for drinking or are you just gonna use it as a hand warmer?

It's a two for one special.

Silvio smiled and wiped an open hand across his forehead. He said, Anyway. I'm a candidate to be a big brother to a kid in the community. I have my volunteer hours at the fire department on Tuesdays, the old-folks home on Wednesdays, the public library on Thursdays, and the animal shelter on Mondays and Fridays. But I can still do more. You don't happen to need any help over at the church do you?

The church isn't so big, Sil. I think I can manage it on my own.

The old man raised the cooled coffee to his lips and drank delicately as his grey eyes peered at Silvio from over the rim of the cup. He said, Anyway, you sound like you are busy enough. It's good to do service for your community. But, Silvio, how is this all going to play out?

What do you mean?

Well, for one, how are you paying the bills?

Silvio straightened his spine and pulled back both of his shoulders in a halfhearted stretching motion. Outside of the diner a large truck pulled into the adjacent parking lot and its tires moved large swaths of water from the low V in the asphalt that acted as the divide between the diner and the truck stop. Waves of displaced water rushed out from the tire base, but after the truck continued on, the water slowly leaked back into the ground's low point and once again sat undisturbed with its oily, gleaming surface. Silvio took a deep breath and then rubbed his right forearm nervously with his opposite hand as he said, I still have some money saved up from my job and from when my parents passed. It's weird for me—I'd like to give money to charity, but if I do that, then I have to go back to work because I don't make any money volunteering. So instead I horde my money from charity, but that hording is what makes me available to volunteer so much. I wish I had a way to just give it all.

You certainly seem to be in the giving mood.

Saints are givers.

The old man only offered a quiet nod of his head. He then said, Your little quest has perked my interest into the whole sainthood thing. It's interesting.

I know.

It's a long, complicated process.

I know.

You'll be long dead before even the possibility of this dream can come true.

I know.

The old man took a content sip of his coffee and couldn't help but smile smugly as he asked, Do you have a couple of miracles up your sleeve, Silvio?

Silvio didn't take notice of the old man's change in tone as he shoveled a forkful of eggs into his mouth. He said, Not that I know of. But I can take care of the miracles after I'm dead.

So, you'll try to be a Confessor of the Faith.

Or a martyr.

The old man nearly spit up his latest drink and didn't attempt to hide the shock on his face and in his response. He said, A martyr? Silvio. . .do you know what a martyr is?

Silvio laughed and said, Of course I do.

Then how could you say something like that?

Silvio shrugged.

The old man tapped his foot nervously. I don't like that, Sil. I don't like that at all. Maybe this is getting out of hand.

The diner was nothing more than a wide version of a trailer home. A big rectangle that Silvio thought, as he looked around it, maybe had indeed once been a trailer home before he shook off the idea and decided it was much too large to ever be hauled behind a vehicle. The southeast corner of the diner was occupied by a large one-skillet kitchen, with the other three walls taken up by booths and windows. Around the kitchen was a bar, and around the bar were chrome-plated stools with vinyl seat covers, where patrons ordered coffee and listened to the sizzle of the skillet that hissed wildly each time the cook pressed onto its contents with the flat of her spatula. She prepared food in short order and plates were delivered as sure as the waitress' shoes clacked quietly on the cheap linoleum tile that had long ago replaced the original carpet everywhere except for under the booths, which the owner was reluctant to tear up. So though the old man's foot tapped fervently at his young friend, its anxiety was lost into the quiet softness of the booth's initial foundation. The waitress came by and asked the old man if he would like more coffee, he would. She asked Silvio if he was still working on his breakfast, he was. When she had moved on to the next table the old man spoke again.

I can't help but think that this whole saint thing is really about something else.

It's not.

Assure me.

Silvio placed the silverware on his plate used the back of his fingers to nudge it toward the middle of the table. He ran a hand through his hair and looked out at the gray clouds and the rain for several seconds. When he finally spoke, his voice was just loud enough to be heard.

A few months ago I was lying in bed, trying to fall asleep. It was so quiet—I didn't think this world could get that quiet anymore. I felt like I had the power of dream without the limits of sleep, and in that silence came to me some purity of thought and everything I could imagine I could feel as if it was real. I could have experienced the whole world in that silence. And of all the thoughts that may have occupied me in that state of mind, my mind turned naturally to God. I began thinking about how I hadn't been to church in so long, and whether or not that was because I didn't believe in God anymore—and even in my heightened space I couldn't know that truth. And so I was consumed by the possibility that he didn't exist.

I thought that I could do something in that room and no one, no thing, would know of it but me. I considered that every evil and benevolent intention I had would never be revealed, let alone judged. Not ever. I considered that every action I made in this life would be trumped by my death and with that death came the end of *me*. No journey for the soul—no growth or transcendence. Nothing. Every daydream and nightmare that I'd ever had was just a product of my brain, and so they would die when my brain did and the decay of them would be no different. Somehow I was able to imagine there was no God and the silence that allowed me to do so settled deep within me. I was an insect. No different than an ant.

Silvio stopped looking at the dark clouds outside and met the old man's eyes of the same color. He had set his coffee cup down during the course of Silvio's monologue but his facial expression had not changed and even now Silvio could draw nothing out of his worn, leathery face. Finally the old man said, Ants are remarkable creatures.

Just an above average organism.

You or the ant?

Silvio shrugged. He picked up his fork and absently pushed at the errant food still on his plate but he ate no more. A waitress glided by on her noisy heels and the old man's leg jittered underneath the table top. Up at the counter, a man placed his order without saying a word. A regular. The shoulders of his flannel shirt were damp from the rain outside and his hat held a host of dirt and stain that settled so deeply into the fabric that to get rid of the filth was to get rid of the hat.

Silvio said, I have never before or since been as afraid as I was in that moment. Until I had truly faced *that* possibility I could not know loneliness. Or maybe I had to do more than face it. I had to soak it in. All the way to my bones.

Silvio shook his head like a man in argument with himself. He said, I heard his voice that night. It said that I won't know it's gone until I realize it was there the whole time. It said that I know nothing of suffering. I found hell in that silence.

Silvio stared out the window for many moments after he had stopped talking. The waitress came by again and took Silvio's plate after being waved off by the old man on her offer of more coffee. Silvio began picking at a fingernail as he continued.

I wasn't right after that. Just empty. I was apathetic at work during the day and afraid to go to sleep at night. All I could think about was that feeling coming back to me. I thought that it'd pass after a few days but it didn't. I thought it'd pass after a few weeks but it didn't. I was worried that if things didn't change quickly then I might be damaged irrevocably.

In a gesture all too familiar to the old man, Silvio shrugged his shoulders and said, It wasn't many days after that when you found me sitting on the church's steps.

The old man nodded his head in remembrance of that moment and snuck a drink of his coffee. He said, Silvio, this thing you're involved in—it can't be for selfish reasons. It can't be about you. It can only be about the people you help. That's it.

I know that, Silvio said.

Are you sure?

Yes. I'm sure.

Okay.

The old man lightly tapped his spoon on the lip of his empty mug. He asked Silvio if he was still writing and Silvio nodded. They both continued to look out the window as the waitresses weaved between booths in their white garb. Young and old they laid their hands on the shoulders of patrons and delivered their checks with smiles and small talk. The backs of the people on the stools remained turned and indifferent to the two who sat quietly in the corner booth. They stared across the counter into the kitchen beyond and at the order wheel that separated them as the light rain continued to branch and split and gather down the cold glass of the window.

So what's next?

Silvio glanced around the diner and said, What do you have say around here to get someone to kill you?

Before 9/11, getting stationed overseas wasn't a big deal for types like me. Someone in my position was most likely to be stationed in a place like Japan, where there hasn't been a conflict related death for years. I'd probably spend twelve-hour night shifts looking at stars through Japan's polluted heavens. But I wasn't that lucky. When commercial flights began attacking America's greatest city, it did more harm to the country's psyche than I could ever comprehend. I experienced the terror and the doubt so common among civilians, and I experienced each of those ten-fold as an enlisted man. When that recruiter at the job fair had so sold me on the virtues of the armed service, I thought about my opportunities to work outside and travel the world. I never considered having to go die alone in the desert under the sun of some country where the people who liked us didn't even like us that much. The recruiter never mentioned that possibility. I don't know if he was trying to dupe me, if there was some quota he was trying to reach, or if he was just as disillusioned as I was before that day. The joke was on me and I had nobody to blame but myself.

In the months that followed the attacks, the energy around the base was decidedly heavier. We stopped horsing around altogether. The smart-ass comments and dirty jokes we so often mumbled under our breath were buried somewhere beneath the rubble in New York City. We were told to be ready, and I stayed up many a night thinking of the possible deployments that loomed in our future. If we got orders to ship off we would only have a couple of weeks' notice. But Thanksgiving rolled around, and then Christmas. By the time Jude showed up in the fall of 2002, it was nearing the one year anniversary of 9/11 and we seemed no closer to finding out if we would see combat or not. Jude's arrival was peculiar, given that he was arriving right when I would've given anything to depart, but, once our friendship blossomed, we began following the exploits of the special forces in Afghanistan as closely as we followed the exploits of NATO and our own U.S. Congress. Within the month, it was common knowledge that special forces had also established a strong presence in Iraq, and whispers of a full-on invasion made their way through the unit.

Reading continued to be a welcome distraction for Jude and I, and, as the holidays came and went again, he opened up more and more about the life he left behind. His story made me feel less sorry for my own situation—he had been gainfully employed, with a college diploma, and was a newlywed. But the thing is, Jude *wanted* to go overseas. He signed up for it. In fact, he didn't enlist until the possibility of going to war became a near certainty. He wanted to enter into the Ranger Indoctrination Program (R.I.P) eventually, but because of his non-existent military background, he was advised to get his feet wet with us. As tensions and plans continued to tighten in a bureaucratic nightmare a universe apart from our own, we mentally prepared to be launched to Afghanistan—where Osama bin Laden was presumed at large. I'll be honest, I couldn't find Afghanistan on a map if my life depended on it. The Middle East was an enigma to me—a place where there was a lot of sand, a lot of sun, and people wore those twisted-cloth hats. Everything I thought I knew about that region was solely based on the imagery of *Aladdin*.

We were forced to wait for three more months before the word was finally given.

War.

Jude was ready. He was itching to be a part of the campaign that brought down the man responsible for those planes. He was ready to win glory, dispense justice, smite his foes, and bring peace to the minds of his fellow Americans. I did my best to live vicariously through Jude in these moments. I tried to fire myself up about Good Guys and Bad Guys, and assure myself that I was aligned with the right ones. I immersed myself, for the first time, in trying to be a good, professional soldier. I was convinced that our mission was a worthy one, and I wanted to see Jude's fulfillment upon its completion. But bad news struck before we even set foot on foreign soil, because we weren't going to Afghanistan—where bin Laden was still thought to be—we were being deployed to Iraq. Now, to me, the only difference between Iraq and Afghanistan is their name. But when we got orders for Iraq, there was a lot of confusion and anger among guys in the unit. Jude was particularly incensed because he had signed up go after Bin

Laden, and by all accounts Bin Laden was in Afghanistan, not Iraq. I finally tracked down a map and, after a fair bit of searching, found that the two countries were quite far apart. I too tried to be upset about this discovery—like I too had been wronged in some way—but I wasn't. I didn't care. There was a war waiting for me in Iraq, and that gave me all the reason I needed to not want to go. The same went for Afghanistan. It didn't matter if we were being deployed to fucking New Jersey, because if there were weapons of mass destruction there, then it was the last place I wanted to be. And just like that, my recommitment to being a good, professional soldier flew out the window. I settled right back into being scared shitless.

I never actually wanted to be in the army, I am a coward by nature, I have a strong leaning toward pacifism, the desert is my least favorite climate type, and still none of these are the best reason for why I should have never set foot in Iraq. Nope. The best reason for why I don't belong in a warzone is my utter lack of instinctual survival skills. I'm always the first one out of a dodgeball match, because I attract high velocity projectiles like a giant magnet. I set the little league record for number of HBP's (hit by pitch). I swim like a cinderblock. It took me two years to learn how to ride a bike because my innate sense of balance is so poor. And, the definitive proof that I didn't stand a chance against guns and explosives, is that I was once nearly killed by a fucking hot dog. It happened about a month out from our deployment date. I hit the small town nearest to our base thirsting for the burn of American whiskey. Most of the guys were visiting hometowns and stopping in on old teachers and girlfriends to make them proud. I had no one to visit and wouldn't have anyways, and so I spent those days raising a quiet but intense drunken hell on that poor town. I vomited on porches and I defecated in gardens and driveways. One night I took out my unit and pissed as I marched down main street, singing *Grand Old Flag*. I like to think that I was just making sure America would remember who died for it—that is, if I did die, and America did have a memory.

On my second to last night of leave, I raged against my circumstance like any doomed man would. I sang Johnny Cash in a bar that didn't offer karaoke and square danced with a lady who lost both of her arms as a child to a rare blood disorder. The bartender eventually kicked me out after I refused to pay my tab. I cited my armed service as worthy compensation, but the bartender wouldn't accept it. He told me to cram my due compensation up my ass, but instead I took it to the local 24/7 store, where that hotdog called out to me like some rotten and forgotten relic from baseball fields and other sentimental Americana.

(A tangential word on Jude and baseball). Jude loved baseball. He was a star shortstop on his high school and college teams and you could ask him anytime what teams or what players were good and he could give you all the specifics. He knew the history of the game and all the statistical leaders of the major categories. I'd watch the occasional game with him and try to keep up with the standings and statistics, but I could never get into it like he did. And he didn't like any of the advanced statistics either, so I stayed away from those. He said that the number geeks were missing the essence of the game—the humanity of it. I had a hard time relating to him because when I played ball as a kid I mostly just got hit by pitches and stood in right field picking my ass while a pack of mosquitos ate me alive. When I think back on it now, the thing that stands out most is the cheap foam liners that they glued inside each helmet. They were supposed to make them fit better and to make them more comfortable but they didn't do either for me—I was only sure of its ability to carry and transmit my compatriots' lice.

In spite of me and baseball's rocky history, I'd still use my computer time to look up the latest news on the Major League season so that I'd have something to talk to Jude about. But it always seemed like the only stories that I could ever find were about something controversial going on in the sport. There'd were endless articles on performance enhancing drugs, appealed suspensions, instant replay, hall of fame voting and asterisks, Pete Rose, the home run king, and so on. I'd just be trying to figure out who the division leaders were—who was good—and all I could ever get was Yankees, Red Sox, and controversies. What a sad sport, I thought, though I never said that to Jude. Its controversies became bigger than the sport itself. The people who covered it were always more concerned with the things going on off the field than they were on it. And everything that was actually happening on the field? It was always tainted by the skepticism of all the people off of it—rightfully so. I figure it's a bad sign when the stuff said about something becomes bigger than the thing itself. Poor baseball. One day, me and Jude got caught up talking about PED's and, Charles overheard us. He must have felt like me, being fed up with all the controversies and such. He says to us that it's appropriate that baseball is still referred to as America's Pastime, because that's all it was. He said the whole situation of the sport was an apt metaphor for our country. I still don't know exactly what he meant by that, but I'll never forget he said it.

Back at the convenient store, I grabbed the oldest looking hotdog there—covered in broils—and soaked it in processed cheese and chili from the nacho machine. I paid for it with my due military compensation, and perched with that dog atop the electrical box to the side of the store. I woke up forty-three minutes later in a hospital bed with the nurse telling me that they had to remove a thumb-sized portion of American sentiment from my throat. I nearly suffocated. Had I actually paid for that hotdog like a civilian, then the cashier would have never called the cops, and I may be just another soldier's corpse in an American parking lot.

When you've figured out how to die to a hot dog, then dying to a gun becomes a walk in the park. I didn't want to go to war. Oh God. If I could die to a hot dog in America . . .

Silvio Submission Three:

BEING GREEK

When I pass into the next life
my family will not place coins upon
my lifeless eye-lids to pay passage
across the river Styx.

I will walk in the mists of some
ethereal shore for a century,
with all the means to my end left behind in the previous world.

A Piece of the Past

He was an unengaged and irreverent single child who replaced the siblings that weren't there for the imaginary friends that were. The ones named Judy and Willard were his favorites, but they constituted only a fraction of a community within his imagination that neither his parents or his fellows at elementary school could comprehend or penetrate. In those formative years, when he took to trouble or found it difficult to make friends at school, he found a certain solace in his mind, and though it held no significance to him then, he learned and kept a lesson that some spend their whole lives witless to—things that aren't real can often be more of a comfort than the things that are.

His adolescent-self adored coming of age stories and they sustained him through those years, only for him to come of age and be as unsure of the world and his place in it as ever. When he found what he thought to be his true-self wading in the muck of his early twenties, it didn't come with a set of convictions and certainties for him to build his life around. While his peers pounded their chests, declared *This is me*, and planted their banners of conquer into the indifferent skin of the world, he came to embrace the ambiguity and the complexity of everything around. And of himself. In spite of this feeling, he became convinced that inside himself lurked some penchant for greatness that he understood to have no tangible origin outside the makings of his own mind. He could think of no other way to explain his desire for such achievements other than the very essence of it seeking him out and lighting within him an acceptance of nothing less. A twenty-first century Pancras searching to invigorate his life in a way that only his death could—forgotten in a time when the period's greatest virtue is the production and preservation of data.

Two years prior to meeting the soldier, the saint was far removed from religion. Despite a spiritual upbringing that involved weekly Bible study with his parents, he fell out of practice the moment he moved away from home. Later, when he challenged himself to recall old Bible passages, he could only bring to mind the time when Jesus advised a grieving son to *Let the dead bury their dead.* Disturbed as he was at that sentiment, he could never again think of the Bible without musing over that very line at least once. *Let the dead bury their dead,* he thought. On his visits home from college, he would attend mass on Christmas Eve and then mass on Easter, and then he wouldn't attend mass on either. But it wore on him, and because he held no more confidence in his faithlessness than he ever did in his faith, he tried to restore some sense of divinity outside of himself. He couldn't. For some time a Quran sat by his bedside, where the intense eloquence of its lullaby would rock him to sleep at night. Soon it was pushed under the bed, alongside a dusty Bible and The Book of Mormon, of which he had made it through Nephite 1.

Those books remained there for over a year before he met her and her faith—her devout faith. He'd make dinner for her while they exchanged memories from their childhoods and dreams from their future. He couldn't help but share things with her that he had thought were vaulted away, and quickly and warily realized he felt about her in a way that he had for no one else before. In spite of this, he recognized the conflict of her beliefs to his soul and, suspecting that neither could be compromised, he tried to terminate their relationship. But he was drawn to her and her to him, and in the late nights of their talking he wasn't afraid to admit that he was in love. Through her, or within her, he rediscovered some semblance of his own faith. He found himself submerged in the most genuine prayers of his life—that he could come to believe what she believed, that he could be worthy of her. On Sundays he would adorn a tie and go with her to feel eyed by the congregation. He thought the transparent motivations for his attendance were as obvious to them as they were to him. A heretic of the worst kind, and nothing but smiles all around.

He knew not if they judged him, but he hated himself for suspecting it. They would strut up to the front of the church one after the other and deliver testimonies as to how they knew God to be God—how they knew the church to be The Church. He bled inwardly during these moments, partly for his own doubts and partly for the pretention of the whole performance. He resented that God was so reductive, and thought that the one real testimony in that building was his endurance of all of this for her. She was his prophet and he her devotee. Every aspect of her was pure religious experience.

He graduated in May of that year and, following a conversation that he could never quite define, he took a job back in his hometown with the implication that she would follow him there soon after. He moved into his parents' basement with short term intentions, and would send her occasional messages on potential living ideas and photographs of the cat he had bought. She hid behind a wall of excuses in regards to moving to his town, and participated in what could only be described as a systematic distancing of herself. Against all the mighty will and effort that he could muster, they grew apart. This was the doom to which he knew their odd romance would always play out, but he was no less hurt when it finally did. He wanted her to be happy, but hoped that the happiness she found would always be tainted by regrets concerning him.

When he was certain that such a person could not exist, she came and lit within him a flame that would not be put out when she was gone, and until his death this reminder, this pinnacle to her, would burn coldly inside of him. He thought heartbreak a term too generally used. His heart was not broken in metaphor or function. Like an apple left to the elements in the field of some forgotten orchard. It wasn't broken, shattered, abused, or torn out of his chest. It just died—a slow and painless recession to the dark place from which all things come. He envisioned himself carrying a symbol not made by or for mankind. Tragic Promethean of a god he stole from her. An act to aid in his own destruction, so as to endure his stone prison for God knows how long.

Had she felt the same way for him, he would have been locked into a life pre-scripted. Working a good job, starting a family, loving her—that would have been his consumption. But in her absence he needed something else to give his life to. Raising a family would no longer be filling his days, and finding a woman who could never live up to her was no benefit.

And in spite of all his mighty work to lid the depositories of his memory, he could not at night control the images that ran feral in his mind. In his sleep were made realities concerning her that never were or would be, and their power alone threatened to consume him entirely. A victim to her or to his own mind he will never know, and to no one will he tell. All those who met him afterward would fail to understand him as only the animate illusion of a spirit deceased. Haunted by potential worlds as distant from them as theirs to him. In his rationalizations hid more questions and within the questions came all the certainties that were broken alongside something unspoken within him. Silvio . . .

MMe and Jude once joked about how we signed our lives over to the government when we enlisted, but we never messed around about how we signed our deaths over too—especially when Iraq escalated. As far as dying goes, if you meet the requirements, a military burial is guaranteed, but not obligatory. Jude, of course, had everything arranged as by-the-book as possible in the case of his expiration—except for one thing (I'll get to that later)—and so I did too. The problem is, after my dishonorable discharge (I'll get to that even later) I was no longer eligible, so it was best if I could get on with not dying. The thing is that the more tangible death became, the more critical it became for those threatened by it to pretend it didn't exist. And that's how most people in the unit addressed it—ignored it—but it's a prospect worth considering, and, in its finality, maybe the most important one to measure.

We hadn't been on base in Iraq for more than a week when Jude approached me in my bunk after hours with a manila envelope in his hand. Ever since word of our deployment reached us, Jude had been pretty low. He knew what he was signing up for, but I don't think there's any way to prepare for something like that. And worse, Jude signed up to fight Osama bin Laden, who as far as we still knew, was an entire country away. I could see how much he missed his wife and the doubt he felt about his decision to enlist. I was torn between trying to be an open ear to his troubles, and easing his pain by trying to remind him of home as little as possible. So on this night, when Jude approached me with the envelope, I was feeling uneasy.

He sat down on my bunk with it held in both hands and it played out just like it does in the movies—he told me to take the envelope, and in the case that something should happen to him, I should make sure it gets to his wife. Inside of it was a letter for her, among other things. I, of course, assured him that this was ridiculous and that nothing would happen to him. In the end, I reluctantly accepted the envelope. He said that all of the relevant details were inside and we never spoke of it again. I hated Jude for giving me that envelope. What's the bird that old sailors were so aware of? The albatross? That's what Jude's gift was to me. I didn't hang it around my neck, but I couldn't help but see it every time I opened the door to my locker, and I couldn't help but feel its weight every time we heard of another American's death.

I had no such thing to give to Jude, and it made me wonder how many soldiers had envelopes like his. And then that single bit of wonder led me down a rabbit hole of wonder that wasn't healthy for a man still in his first month of a yearlong deployment. How many envelopes were out there like Jude's? How many of those envelopes and letters were responsible for delivering the last sentiments of men and women, never to be heard again? And how many of those envelopes were prepared and never made it to their destination? They were lost wishes buried alongside the very men who dared to wish them at times that mocked the very idea of it.

And I'm not just talking American soldiers either. What about the Iraqi soldiers, or freedom fighters, or whatever it is they were calling themselves? They must have had plenty of their own Jude's, and Iraq was losing them at a more sickening rate than we were. And, since I had already gone down the hole as far as I did, how could I not think about all the civilians that were being killed? What about all those people that didn't sign up for anything and didn't get the opportunity to leave behind so much as a good-bye? And there were *a lot* of civilians caught in the middle. Nearly three-thousand people died in the attacks of September 11, and that is one of the great tragedies in American history—a scar that will never be forgotten so long as America is America. Nearly three thousand people . . . And yet when things really escalated in Iraq in 2003, Iraqi civilian casualties were estimated at around twelve thousand for the year. *Four times* the amount of Americans that died in one of the most horrific moments in my country's history. And that's just one year—they've had worse. Also, that's an *estimate*. Their lives are so fleeting, and lost at such an intense and chaotic rate, that it's nearly impossible to pin down an exact number. If 9/11 is one of America's great scars, how many scars does Iraq have? How many scars can one body have before there is no healthy cells for the scar tissue to latch on to? What then?

Jude often questioned what we were doing there, and why we weren't in Afghanistan. I didn't have any answers for him, and the soldiers who were asking the same questions didn't have answers either. The blow-shit-up-guys were happy to have the opportunity to blow shit up, the Jude guys were struggling to justify their ideals on individual levels, and the guys like me were just counting the days until we could go back home. My greatest hope was that our shock and awe campaign succeeded in shocking and aweing and I could spend my deployment like I was supposed to—night duty, star gazing, and so on—but I wasn't that lucky. *We* weren't that lucky. Only five weeks after arriving on base, my unit was about to give the shock and awe treatment as well as we got it.

The mission was supposed to be a routine one. We were doing escort duty for a maintenance company near the outskirts of some city that I have as good of a chance at spelling correctly as I do at pronouncing it. It was a large city, and we wouldn't dare go to the heart of it, but the brass was sure we could go around it with no problem. As we skirted the edge of the city and crossed a bridge, our lead Humvee was hit and disabled by an RPG, and in a matter of seconds the other three Humvees and four tracs that made up our company were barraged by fire from nearby rooftops and al-leyways. The Iraqi's weren't exactly bringing heavy firepower on us at first, but we were caught completely off guard. Our debrief had informed us that the locals were going to treat and celebrate us as liberators, not invaders. I believed them too. Why wouldn't I? It wasn't until later that I thought about the notion of us as liberators. What if Iraq sent its army overseas to America with the purpose of overthrowing the President and scouring the country-side for our most effective weapons? And what if a very small contingent of that invading army decided it was going to capture a bridge just outside the city of Boston or, say, Chicago? Would they be treated as liberators? I'm capable of imagining the hell that would be unleashed in that scenario, but I don't need to, because I saw it that day in Iraq.

Once word had gotten out that some Americans were pinned down nearby, it seemed like every Iraqi with a gun came out of the woodwork for his or her chance to take down the most powerful military on the face of the earth. They swarmed toward our caravan mostly with old Karishnakovs and hand guns of who knows what make and model. It's like they just dug all that shit out of some old cache from the Gulf War years, or from some other war one-hundred years before that. The majority of them didn't even bother to take cover from us—they just stood out in the open, screaming and pumping their guns into the air as much as they shot them at us. The great mob of them with so much anger and those that didn't have guns would curse as they threw rocks and bottles. In some cases they might as well have had pitchforks. Occasionally the front line of the mob, which had worked itself to within fifteen yards of us at some points, would surge toward us like a rising tide, fire a few rounds or throw a few rocks, and then retreat to the original line. It was like we were playing the most violent game of dodgeball you could imagine. It was a form of warfare that I never could have imagined—the sharp ricochet of bullets hitting the tracs and Humvees, the thud of them hitting the turf around us, the shouting of soldiers, the roaring of the mob, and the cries of the wounded from both sides.

I'll never forget the dud RPG's they were firing at us. One of them hit the side of our trac not six feet from my head and bounced off about a dozen yards into the desert behind us and never exploded. First Sergeant Murphy saw that same RPG and said to me, We're up shit creek now.

I didn't say anything.

By this time another Humvee had taken severe damage from another RPG and its hood was on fire from a homemade fire cocktail. It didn't look like we were going anywhere. I lost Jude as soon as the initial engagement took place, but he was next to me now—in the kneeling position firing around the corner of the trac, and me standing, firing blindly over his head. I still don't know if I hit anyone or anything with my sporadic fire—I'd get my muzzle around the corner of the trac and pop off a few rounds before returning to my relative safety.

It seemed like it would go on forever, but comprehensive orders finally reached us—not that they changed our situation. We were told that a company of marines were on their way to give us relief and get us the hell out of there. The rest of their story I didn't hear until later, when we made it back to base. That company, consisting of about two-hundred marines, riding in three Humvees and a dozen tracs, were supposed to get to us, lay down some serious Devil-Dog-wood and escort us back to base. But, on their way to our besieged company, the marines wisely decided to not drive up the same road we did. Instead, they swung around on a route even closer to edge of the city, where the population thinned out. This was solid logic—solid logic ruined by a stroke of bad luck. As the unit crept along the backside of the city toward our location, they came to a salt flat in which they got stuck. It turned out that what looked like a salt flat was really just a swamp where much of the sewage from the city was funneled and inadvertently covered by a layer of sunbaked mud. When the tracs rolled into that quagmire, it was like a tyrannosaurus rex walking into a tar pit—the harder they tried to get out, the deeper they dug themselves in. It didn't take long for word to get out among the Iraqis about another group of Americans pinned down nearby. The Iraqis swarmed to them just as they did to us, and their situation became just as dire.

We were fighting for our lives, keeping the Iraqi horde at bay, and dragging wounded soldiers into the most protected trac. When they'd cry out for their mothers, it took everything I had to not to despair. I felt like the Marine Company was taking forever to get to us, but I had no sense of time, or sense of anything. Jude was still with me, now covering the opposite end of our trac as we continued to lose more and more soldiers to our improvised hospital. I'll never forget the sound of the jets coming our way—the roar of those beautiful birds. The Iraqis only had jets like that in their wildest dreams, and so that sound could only come from American jets, and we knew it. Superiority through air power.

I kept mumbling, Oh, thank God. Oh, thank God, while Private Church was next to me and he started squealing, What the fuck. What the fuck.

The next thing I knew, a few minor explosions set off all around the convoy and a string of bullets hit the dirt around me at an ungodly rate. Whatever was firing them was doing it so fast that it sounded like a buzz-saw fit for the hands of Paul Bunyan. I couldn't figure out what on earth the Iraqis had gotten their hands on, when someone screamed, Oh, Jesus. They're shooting the wrong people.

Even after hearing that, it took me a few seconds to realize we had just been blown halfway to Hell by our own air force. And where was Jude? Where was Jude? Oh, Jesus, they're shooting the wrong people.

The world stopped moving for what seemed like minutes. I was sitting on my ass and I couldn't remember how I'd gotten there. I couldn't hear or see anything, but it appeared that the arrival of our air force had caused the mob to scatter. Great surges of dirt and gunpowder filled the air around me and I began to reflexively pat at my limbs to see if I was missing any. I felt all around my body like a blind man does and then held my hands inches to my face to inspect for blood. I didn't see anything. I rolled over to push myself off the ground and began calling through the dirt for survivors.

God only knows how we eventually got out of there. I was one of the few people who wasn't harboring any serious physical injury, but I can't recall a single memory between the air strike and when we finally made it back to base. The air force finally got their shit together on who the enemy was and we ditched the torched vehicles in order to get off the bridge. What a tragedy . . . Later it was explained to me that in the heat of battle some soldiers would click on their radios to relay orders and then forget to turn them off. They called it hot miking and it could jam up communication for hours. It explained why it took so long for our unit to get relief. It explained why, in their own critical situation, the bogged down Marine Company called in an airstrike on a group of hostile vehicles north of it, assuming we were long gone at that point. It explained how the Air Force might accidentally strafe a friendly caravan too. But it couldn't explain the Iraqi people, and why they were killing us instead of celebrating us. It couldn't explain why we were in a different country than Osama Bin Laden. And it couldn't explain where Jude was. Where was Jude, God dammit? It couldn't explain where the fuck Jude went.

Nothing could.

Between Jude and the trench knife, I was in no position to liberate some country whose inhabitants seemed set on killing me. After a blitz of psychological evaluations, I was deemed unfit for combat and scheduled to return back home for further processing and therapy. Whatever. I went into Iraq believing at least I could fight for the man next to me—fight for Jude. But when the man next to me was obliterated by the man next to him—by American angels smiting troops from the heavens? I couldn't do that. They could go fuck themselves. I was giving them no more of me—Jude had already given enough for both of us.

Silvio Submission Four:

ACHILLES

You are awake and you are asleep
and then your body is buried
a distance underground as arbitrary
as the experience that headlined
your epoch of utter forgetability.

The lucky ones travel as far
as a donated bench on the decaying lawns
of a country club tennis court—
an epitaph carved among the stones of millions.

Achilles' legacy was carved by the sword
and perpetuated by the pen,
each as mighty as the man wielding it—
the idea of a man as told by another man's idea.

You wouldn't know him in the afterlife.
You wouldn't even recognize him
if you crossed paths on the street.

Rigor Mortis

In the cavity of her post-departure he was prone to play out entire romances in his mind. He would introduce himself to women and flirt with them enough to bait out a response he thought worthy of his efforts, and then sulk quietly back into his isolation. While there, he would turn his flirt into a paragon to rival *her*. The first date would unravel with the nervous tension true to the occasion—a role in which he would be just charming enough, and her just sweet enough, to grant him a second date. Even in his fantasies he could not muster the courage for a kiss during those first encounters.

The second date never held the status or the ritual of the first, and so his mind moved on quickly to the point where their weekend dates were pre-scripted and she would spend no less than two nights a week in his bed. Her skin would be flawless, her humor clever, and her not-really-skeletons-in-the-closet skeletons were bared honestly. Her parents were always the All-American type—teachers and firefighters and small business owners who couldn't help but want to adopt him as their own. She'd have siblings who would embrace him into the fold too—brothers who would ask him to watch baseball and play video games with them at Thanksgiving, and younger sisters who would giggle and blush anytime he wasn't looking.

When she became perfect he would be forced to push her away for reasons that were vague and not altogether important within these non-realities. In his mind, he was baptized by fire. A figure too wounded for love, and so he must push away her that dared to do so. She would always think of him as a compelling and limitless phantom, while he took solace in his duty to navigate her to someone without the burden of his wounds. He needed to end love for the sake of love. He saw himself setting her free by transferring the sins of her affection onto his already clipped wings. A romantic who knew no romance and wouldn't bother to. Wild Hamlet whose tragedies played out on the stage of his mind alone—all of this born from one girl who he talked to for ten minutes during the intermission of a play and never saw again.

He continued living out of his parents' house because they gave him his space, and he bought a kitten from the litter of a fellow employee and he would spend nights petting its soft back and appreciating its lack of desire to show him any affection in return. He named the cat Saint Francis and whenever he pushed it from his lap it would go to the opposite end of his room and stare at him with great intrigue, and when he looked into its grey and green-speckled eyes he was never sure of what he saw there. At work he went through the motions and his savings account swelled from living off of his parents' coin, but this did little for him because he saved toward nothing of significance and lusted dully for material objects. He made two trips back to the town of his college, and while there he lingered in the places that he knew her to frequent. It had been months since they last talked and he wouldn't dare call her now. He acted casually and naturally, but she never showed up to the places he crept and the routine he had so diligently worked in regards to approaching her was never put to the test. He never saw her and he never asked about her. He would never talk to her again for the duration of his life.

For the next year he continued working and saving, and at night Saint Francis would sit atop his bookshelf and lock his grey eyes onto Silvio and not move them for hours. What little was held together for him fell apart on a Tuesday morning in September. He was watching the morning news and he had just seen what he thought to be a human body fall from a burning skyscraper when the phone rang. The voice on the other end of the line asked for his name and the names of his parents. As the ungodly amount of smoke and fire rose out of the tower stack and through the television onto his glassy eyes, the voice on the phone told him that there had been a car accident and he was needed at the hospital where a pair of sheriff's deputies would take him to identify and say one last goodbye to his parents. They said how sorry they were to deliver the news and he said nothing. In the basement of the hospital, a deputy asked him if he wanted to know what happened, and when he started talking of rain and a deer in the road, Silvio cut him short and told him, That's enough. He spent no more than a minute searching for an oddity in their death that might lend itself to some higher meaning, but his father was retired and his mother was mostly retired, and to take a Tuesday morning to drive to a nearby town with the area's best home repair store was nothing to decipher. Maybe the plane too was just another crash, another accident. It was easy enough to do with all the rain and the deer and the fire. Maybe in trying to avoid one tower, it had hit the other. His focus turned to calling family members, but that lasted as long as it took for a nurse let out a cry of despair and cover her mouth with her hands as she watched another 767 land into the glass exoskeleton of the second tower. He placed the phone down gently and took a seat in the hospital's deeply-bowled plastic chairs that were cast in the most unnatural shade of orange. The television he watched was old and sat elevated in the far corner of the room on a metal arm. Its images were small and blurred, which made the great black smudge of smoke even more sinister in his mind. The voice of his mother was in his head and it urged him to focus on the people that were helping, and though the smoke was the prevalent monster on the screen, he turned his attention to the hundreds that ran *toward* the fires. There was a little bit of hero in so many people and look how readily they dove into harm's way as if their whole lives they wanted to be more and now in this tragedy came their moment. He didn't leave the hospital's basement for hours, and though he had never been to New York City he could, by the end of the day, identify nearly every building of its skyline on sight. Every face he saw was looking up because the only people who could take their eyes from it were the ones running away—those cast in ashen skin and seared eyes. They burned and they raged and they smoked and who could have guessed that they hadn't yet seen the worst of it. When the first tower collapsed he rose from his chair in equilibrium to the incalculable weight of concrete and steel that crashed down, and it was the only moment of the day that he briefly forgot that his parents were dead, and how many more? There were tear stains down his cheeks but he couldn't blink and his eyes dried out but he couldn't stop watching. He watched and he watched and when the sun went down and a hospital staffer told him that he needed to go home, he left his car in the parking lot. He sold it privately and never drove it again.

He walked home and would walk anywhere else he needed to go. He contacted family members and there was a rainy funeral a week later. He thought he had once heard that it's a good omen to have it rain on the funeral day of the departed, but he took no solace in it. His family eventually retreated back to their corners of the world and he was left in the empty home of his parent's life. On most nights he cooked a frozen dinner and ate it in his room in the basement, while Saint Francis challenged him with those big grey eyes that offered nothing.

When I was a kid I would raise a lot of hell with fireworks. I'd latch bottle rockets onto the tails of neighborhood cats, get into roman candle wars with friends, and line the spokes of my bike with smoke bombs and sparklers. But anthills were my favorite targets. Nothing gave me pleasure like cramming an M-80 into an anthill and, in one moment, seeing the top of their big sand cones fractured like you see a mountain peak after it decides it's a volcano. I would never do that again now. Now that I've been the ant I can't see any beauty in it. I just wish I could go back to that moment in Iraq and keep it all intact. If I were God that's what I'd do—I'd pluck that rocket out of the air and flick it out into space. At least that way it wouldn't take my friend into space with it. And steal childhood love of explosions. And turn me into an ant.

When our caravan was strafed by our own air support, I couldn't have been more than fifteen feet from Jude on the other end of the trac. He was lucky enough to avoid the badass blender of machinegun fire, but not the small rocket barrage that came with it. The rocket that hit his end of the trac sent time and sound and Jude's life into an irretrievable and infinite amount of directions, leaving me in a vacuum null of them all. I don't know where they came to settle at, but I bet if I ever find my way back to that desert, I'm just as likely to find pieces of that moment as I am grains of sand.

I can't properly say that I've gotten any more than a glimpse into the ugly maw of war, because I was involved in a single battle, and some might not even call it that. Really, I was just on the wrong end of the Boston Massacre—a scared shitless soldier surrounded by a principally angered mob. But that one experience was more than enough for me. It was so god damn scary. My uncle Corbin used to say there were many forms of bravery, and that there were many forms of cowardice. But if in me there was cowardice, then my cowardice was born from meaning, and my bravery in its recognition. Because deciding to get one last look at Jude's body was maybe the bravest thing I've ever done. I'm not sure why I felt so compelled to see him one last time, but I know that cowards don't look into the faces of the dead. His body was packaged up in a big hangar with six other bodies set neatly in a row, and my hand shook as I peeled back the plastic bag zipped around him. The left side of his face was disturbingly intact, and the right side was still in the desert, or in space, or somewhere before the moment of that rocket. Kind of like I am—somewhere before that moment, with the ants, the sand, and an appreciation for life.

During my time in the service I kept all the cynical viewpoints to myself. I never told anyone how I felt about the trench knife, about killing and dying, about why the hell we weren't in Afghanistan—not even Jude. I kept telling myself in my head that this is what I signed up for and I was going to deal with it. Besides, no one wants to be that person who just complains about circumstances that they're either totally in control of, or events that are just the opposite. If you asked the people I served with they'd likely tell you that I was a good soldier, because they'd be too nice to tell you that I was mediocre at best. I shut my mouth while I went about my below average business. Because of this, I felt real shame in being ordered home, despite recognizing the inability to do my job effectively. I was abandoning my company in spite of being physically capable of doing my duty, if not psychologically. But the brass' diagnosis was that if we got into another conflict, it was unpredictable how I would respond and that I'd likely do more harm than good. In some cases they may have found something for me to do on the base that had a lower chance of seeing combat, but that didn't solve the issue of me keeping my barracks up all hours with constant night terrors that came in nearly every dream after that disastrous mission.

I caught a ride back to the states in a large cargo plane that was scheduled to hop across the pond after only one refuel. I slept as much as I could, but my mind was distracted and it constantly drifted to what else must be stashed around the plane. I wondered if Jude was on it with me—boxed like another piece of cargo, a folded American flag. At some point over the Atlantic, I woke up to what seemed like an abnormal engine noise. The plane dropped fast enough to lift my stomach into my mouth, and when we leveled off again, the engine sounded twice as loud as before. I gripped tightly onto the harness that came down across both of my shoulders and looked around in the dark belly of the plane. I had been alone for the entire ride, so it shouldn't have been a surprise that I saw nobody, except that, for some reason, it *was* a surprise, and I started to panic. My breathing accelerated and I called out into the dark cabin. Who was flying this thing? Where were we? A uniform appeared in the dim light at front end of the cargo hold and called out to me to fasten my belt. I was breathing heavily and dark spots soon gathered at the edge of my vision. I wanted to get up to see what was going on, but I was too afraid to move. I recalled that, other than a brief hand shake when I boarded, I didn't know any of the crew on the plane. Who were they? How could I be sure that they were actually American Air Force? The image of a plane flying into a skyscraper was running through my mind and the roar of the engine magnified while I gripped and clawed at my seat harness as I fought for air. I screamed wildly into the darkness around me. I was sure that our plane was on the verge of something very bad happening when the guy in the uniform appeared again and attempted to calm me down. He convinced me that the turbulence was normal and that he was indeed a member of the Air Force. He harnessed himself in next to me, told me to take deep breaths, and I was still gasping for air when he started telling me a story. It took place while he was in boot camp, and it was about a service member in the same boot who was a total screw up. The guy would never show up on time for anything, he would fail to meet proper dress standards, and he would forget to appropriately address superior officers. Finally, their squad leader pulls the screw up aside and, after a good yelling, tells the soldier to wait right where he is. The squad leader disappears out of the barracks and comes back about ten minutes later carrying this little potted tree with him. The squad leader shoves the little tree into the poor guy's chest and says to him, *You will keep this tree alive. You will carry it with you every moment you are in uniform. You will take it to PT, you will take it to chow, you will take it to work. If anyone asks you why you're carrying this fucking tree around, you will tell them, "It's to replace the oxygen I stole from everybody else."*

By the time he got to the punch line, my breathing had almost returned to normal. I even managed a little laugh at the expense of that poor soldier. The Air Force captain unlatched his harness, stood up, and patted me on the near shoulder. He said that I should get some rest and that we'd be stateside before I knew it. He walked back across the dim belly of the plane and I fell into a dreamless sleep.

Soon after we landed back at base in Georgia, I got worked into a routine with another company, and with a therapist's couch. I told the therapist about Jude, but about little else. I mostly just dodged his questions and kept my mouth shut because I didn't want to be there. I told him that I liked reading and so he recommended that I read as often as I could. I took him up on his advice, but I now considered myself retired from the Fantasy genre, and so I went to the base's library to find something a little different. What I ended up with was a non-fiction account of the American Civil War, which, ironically, gave me the final, psychological push that I needed to leave the service. Here's what I read, more or less:

General Robert E. Lee was an absolute stud of a general, a real leader of men. Without his significant talents at the head of the Confederate army, I probably wouldn't have bothered to read this account of the Civil War in the first place—there wouldn't have been any account *to* read. The war would have taken up three sentences in your eighth-grade history book. *The Southern States secede. The Confederate Army is annihilated. America is fine.* But that's not the way it happened, mostly because the South had this guy, Lee, who was such a good General that the conflict dragged on for four years. And then Lee was forced to surrender on April 9, 1865. That was it. The war was over. Except that the war wasn't *really* over, because other generals in other parts of the country decided they were going to keep fighting. Despite losing the war in every way imaginable, their most prestigious general surrendering himself and his army, and having exactly a zero percent chance of defeating the Union, those generals and the Confederate president decided that they were going to keep on fighting. And that was the final straw between me and military service. Because the moment before Lee surrendered, those Southern boys were fighting with a *purpose*—misguided though it was. The moment after his surrender? They were just murderers. Purposeless killers. Most of them probably didn't realize it, but that's the point. A few strokes of ink by a man a few hundred miles away transformed their acts of bravery into ones of lunacy. General Lee's surrender transformed soldiers into mercenaries, and martyrs into men.

They were killing each other in the backwoods of America for an outcome that had already been decided. When I finished reading I couldn't decide where the bigger tragedy lied—with those who were murdered after the war was officially over, or with those that died within days, before or after, of the surrender. And why stop there? Somewhere within those hills or on the streets of some city lies the bones of a man who was casualty number one. Somewhere next to him, or very far away, lies casualty number 236, 414. And is the value of a man buried at Gettysburg greater than that of one that fell on a lesser battlefield? What meaning does a soldier's death have when what he fights for is already won? Is it any different for when he's already lost?

Holy shit, I don't know. I don't know what it takes to have a life of meaning, and I certainly don't know the nature of that meaning when you sign up to kill people. The talk is always about dying for your country, but what it really comes down to is a willingness to kill for it. Ask any young man who signs up for duty if he expects to die. Does he? Hell no. Does he expect to have to kill anybody? If that's what it takes. He is fucking immortal. Everyone knows they'll die, just nobody believes it.

It took some stupid book for me to recognize I didn't sign up for killing or dying. If I was going to be killing people, then I wanted to be sure that I wasn't a murderer, and I saw no way to do that. I could never be confident that in a room, thousands of miles away, someone wasn't making a decision that would disqualify everything I had done with a patch on my arm. I couldn't have some obscure political arrangement made by two people that I had never met transforming me from a hero into a sociopath. And if that makes me a coward, then so be it. I'm not against war, but I sure as hell am not going to die in one.

The Fiction of Strangers

S he hid behind the glow of her cigarette as if the pale smoke of its burning could veil her from the activity around the public library. She slowly drew the poison into her slight frame as she watched figures hauling books, like merchants from some market square that deals only in paper and words and the fiction of strangers. As Silvio walked by her bench he waited for her to glance up so offer a greeting, but she didn't. She continued to stare off at distant specters moving in the early summer and wondered how they could somehow enjoy the sunny mid-morning while she continued to slowly kill herself. In the library he read to a small group of children from a small chair set on a brightly dyed rug. As he turned the page where the caterpillar transforms into a butterfly, he noticed her pushing a cart of books around the library's stacks. When the story was over, he found her running a hand over the spines of a row of books near one of the back shelves. He offered her a greeting and she responded with a dismissive smile.

He asked, Are you new here?

I'm a volunteer, she said.

Silvio grinned and said, I am too.

A sarcastic smile from her.

He said, So do you just stack books?

I do whatever they ask me to do.

You should see if you can read to some of the kids. It's fun.

Who are you?

I'm Silvio.

Well, *Silvio*. . .I don't think they want me reading to a group of kids.

Why not?

Because I'm not a *volunteer* volunteer.

He shook his head and said, I don't understand.

I'm here because I have to be.

You have to be?

That's what I just said, isn't it?

Why do you have to be?

What are you? The volunteer police?

If I was, then you wouldn't be a concern to me.

What are you talking about?

Well if you *have* to be here then you aren't much of a volunteer, and if you aren't a volunteer then I imagine you are out of the jurisdiction of the volunteer police. Although, to be fair, I'm not terribly familiar with the inner workings of their organization.

She gave him a deadpanned stare for a moment, then she shook her head as she read the flap of the next book in her cart before shelving it on the bottom row.

He said, Do you mind if I ask why you are forced to be here?

If I do mind, are you going to ask anyway?

I won't ask.

She looked at him with her head tilted. She met his eyes and then turned back to a new book in her hand.

She said, I'm ordered by the court to be here. I got into trouble awhile back and volunteering one-hundred hours was part of my sentencing.

Silvio gave a non-committal nod.

Drunk driving—you're going to ask anyway.

Another nod.

She kept her eyes forward on the shelf, sliding a book home into its cataloged space and evaluating the call number of the next one on her cart. Silvio pretended to browse in the same aisle as he analyzed her profile out of his peripheral. Her jeans and blouse fit tightly around her delicate frame, and her thick, dark hair was pulled back into a ponytail.

Silvio said, Libraries are weird places, you know?

I didn't know.

Silvio nodded. He grabbed a book off the shelf and spun it in his hand and said, Most of these books are the life achievements of a lot of different people. People you and I have never even heard of. Certainly they all had dreams of writing a truly *great* novel, but so few of them could. I wonder, had they been able to envision the lackluster reception of their work, if they would have bothered at all.

She had stopped sorting through the books on her cart and said, I would've.

Yeah?

Yeah, she said. I mean, if there were just one person who read my book and really enjoyed it, then that would be amazing. That would be all I needed.

Silvio nodded again and fanned the pages of the book in his hand. He stared at its front cover for a second then put it back in its place on the shelf. She continued analyzing the call numbers when she said, I've seen you before you know.

Silvio regarded her again as if he had forgotten she was there. He said, I *didn't* know. How come I've never seen you before?

It's a big town.

No its not.

She let out a short laugh which she tried to stifle with one of her hands.

She said, At that church—the brick one. I live right across the street. I've seen you outside there before.

That sounds like me.

Why do you spend so much time there?

I volunteer there too—writing mostly.

You must be pretty bad at this whole volunteering thing.

What?

I had a coach who once told me that if someone does something for free it's probably because they aren't any good at it.

Silvio looked at her full on now and said, I can't tell if you are messing with me or not.

I can't either.

He said, Maybe sometimes it's just good to do something for other people, but I don't need to tell that to a fellow volunteer do I?

She said, I deserved that.

Silvio smiled and plucked a book that he hadn't even looked at from the shelf in front of him. He acted as if he had found what he came for and preceded toward the front of the library.

Before he rounded the corner of the stack she said to him, Thanks for making me laugh. It's been a rough couple of months.

Silvio turned back to her and asked if everything was okay.

I'll be fine, I think.

Silvio nodded. He said, If you ever need someone to talk to, you should stop by the church sometime—I could show you around.

Only if you promise to write something for me.

He turned the corner of the shelf and said back to her, Only if you promise to pay for it.

Silvio Submission Five:

BAAL

A subtle thunderstorm in the high
plains that are not quite mountains—
those lie in the near distance,
shown under the empty black sky by divine light.
Atop that mountain may be a storm
god with the privilege to be witnessed
more than any other god since he carved
his throne atop that peak with whatever
gods carve with: sheer will?
However, this is not the storm god that
will screw your spouse in your disguise—
this one only asks for the blood of
first born sons, or a surrogate sacrifice
for those with money enough
to fool his intentions.

Back in the States, I ditched the base at the front end of a three day leave in order to give myself the biggest head start possible. I drew three-thousand dollars from two different cards at two different ATM's and rid myself of everything that marked me as a soldier, and everything that marked me as me. I hit up a store for outdoorsman and picked up a fifty-liter backpack and a mummy sleeping bag. I roamed among the store's mannequins and settled on a pair of canvas pants that had a zip-off lower leg—they were as stupid looking as they were practical. I threw a package of undershirts and underwear into the bag, and then picked out a flannel sweater to help with the cold nights. I got me a waterproof jacket for obvious reasons, and then finished up with several nice pairs of crew hiking socks and pair of dura-leather hiking shoes. I didn't know what the protocol was for a deserter, but I knew that they wouldn't even know I was a deserter for a couple more days, and in that time I could use more traditional means of travel. I splurged for a cab ride to Atlanta and hopped on an Amtrak that took me through Birmingham to Jackson, Mississippi. I held no ties to this part of the country and so I figured if they ever did start looking for me, then the South would be last place they ever would. Comforted by this logic, I evaluated my options.

The fact that I hit the point of no return without the slightest notion of a plan was proof enough of my mental state. I was a psychological disaster. But in Jackson, I gave myself some semblance of direction. First, I was determined to be a vagabond. I'd only use what money I had when my survival depended on it, because I had no idea how long I'd have to make those three-thousand dollars last. Second, I'd absolutely have to stay away from jail, or from anything involving the authorities. I'd have to watch where I slept, and where I mingled, in order to dissuade any unwanted attention.

Third, if I couldn't hitchhike, then I'd walk. The going would be slow, but I didn't have anywhere to be, so this aspect didn't concern me. Lastly, by the time winter came, I'd either be on the west coast or somewhere in the Southwest, where it was warm. What I was going to do from there only God knows.

Jackson was hot and humid, and I walked northeast through the town with a mind to seeing how the rest of the world reacted to my new identity. They didn't. To my relief, I was met with the same indifference I always had been. It was as if I hadn't just been through the most harrowing experience of my life, as if I hadn't just abandoned my post in the world's most powerful army, as if it really were just a hot summer day in need of a little bit of shade and a cold drink. When I looked around me I didn't see a country that was at war. I saw a place where war is an abstract concept that can be debated and politicized, but it wasn't a place that kept caches of old RPGs and assault rifles on the off chance that a foreign invader attempts to cross a nearby bridge.

I was nervous about my first night on the streets, so I walked with the purpose of finding a good spot to sleep. My avoidance of major roads corralled me into the northeastern portion of the city, and after a few hours I encountered a river. My first thought was that it must be the iconic Mississippi river. It wasn't. I quickly realized it was too small to be the Mississippi and my suspicions were confirmed shortly after as I saw signs for the Pearl River. I crept north along the river's shoreline and it was clear that I was far from the first person to look for shelter here. There were tents. There were sleeping vagrants. There were fragments of trash being pushed up into the river's shoreline atop the mild current. The vegetation grew thicker as I followed it north and, sheltered by a swath of large cordgrass and spindly little willow, I found a suitable place to camp out. I wasn't the first one to find the small cove—there were empty chip bags, crushed water bottles, unidentifiable plastic scraps, and a cleared spot on the ground about the size of a sleeping human body. I kicked aside most of the garbage and sat against the small willow and the meager shade it provided. The summer sun wouldn't be going down for a while longer, but I settled in anyway and fell asleep almost instantly.

I was startled awake by several explosions, and I was severely disoriented as large flares filled the night sky above me and everything around me took on their red, murky glow. Then I heard gunfire to the south of me. To the west of me, more flares. More red. I scampered into the cordgrass, went full fetal position while covered my ears, and in my panicked state tried to piece together what was going on. Was I Still in Iraq? Had the war come to the states? Had the Army discovered my desertion and come looking for me?

The rational part of my brain attempted to kick in and settle me down, but after another burst of nearby gunfire I dipped deeper into the panic and confusion. I could feel the hot desert wind on my face. I could see the dud RPG's ricocheting off Humvee doors. I could hear the doom of fighter jets racing toward me in their state of disorganized violence. My head was filled with images of Jude's dead face, and tears began to run down mine. I heaved desperate breaths of air for several minutes and waited for whatever this red chaos was to put me out of my misery, but the killing blow never came. I stayed balled up for several more minutes before a familiar whistling pulled me out of the fog in my head. I knew that whistling. It didn't come from any RPG, rifle, or F-16 fighter jet—it came from a firework. The exact same kind I used to play with as a kid. Given everything that had happened in my life in the previous few months, I had lost all track of time and had no idea that it was July 4th already. I was still shaken up, but my breathing steadied. Another barrage of firecrackers went off nearby, but I was stable now. I sulked back to my original spot under the tree, embarrassed and exhausted, and did my best to appreciate the rest of the festivities before falling asleep again—this time through the night.

I took the fireworks to be a bad omen for me, and the next morning I made my way, by foot, as quickly as possible toward highway 55. I found myself in some pretty tough neighborhoods and thought about the cash that I had on my person, but, like the previous day, I was largely ignored. When I hit 55, I walked north alongside it until I hit what I thought was a suitably busy on-ramp. It only took two hours of baking in the Southern sun before a truck driver hollered at me to jump in, and I was on my way to Tennessee.

It wasn't until this long stretch of freeway between Jackson and Memphis, riding shotgun in that semi-truck, that I thought about the envelope that Jude handed me in Iraq. The sudden memory of having it sent me into a near panic. The driver, an overweight woman, asked me if I was on drugs, and, through my heavy breathing, I assured her that I was not. I patted quickly at the outside of my pack and, after searching through four zippered compartments, found the envelope that contained Jude's letter. I gripped it tightly in my hand. My breathing immediately subsided and the driver asked me, Did you find your drugs there?

I told her again that I didn't do drugs, and she began laughing at me. She was screwing with me. She said she could spot a drug user from a mile away, because her husband used to drive rigs with her and he had gotten into amphetamines to help get him through long hauls. He was dead now and I said I was sorry to hear it, but she dismissed me with a wave of her hand and mumbled something under her breath. After we drove on for several more hours she told me that she couldn't take me past Memphis, which was no issue to me since Memphis was just as good as the next place. When we arrived on the fringes of the city she pulled into a busy truck stop and I readied myself to depart. As she was fueling and I was thanking her for picking me up she said, In twelve years of driving I've never picked up a single person looking for a ride from the side of the road. Too many weirdos. Too dangerous. You know why I picked you up? Because even at fifty-five miles per hour you stood out like a sore thumb. Your clothes are clean—new, even. Your hair's still got a cut to it. You've had a shower more recently than I have. I just had to stop, and I wanted to figure out what you were doing out on the side of that highway. But I knew right away that you wouldn't be telling me anything. I saw it in your eyes as soon as you climbed up in the cab. I see it in your eyes now, and the only way I can explain it is that you're carrying something bad down in you. Kid, I don't know what you got going on, but I just feel the need to tell you to hang in there. Okay? Whatever you're running from or whatever you did, it's not so bad.

I didn't know what to say to her, so I just nodded my head and thanked her again for the ride. It was already late afternoon and I immediately took to finding a place where I could spend the night without drawing any attention to myself. The driver's words about how much I stood out had spooked me and so I took the first opportunity I had to roll around in a dirt lot. I must have looked crazy as fuck just rolling around in the dirt, but I had to scuff up before the wrong people started making observations.

I skirted the interstate for two more hours before I reached a major traffic hub and decided to take refuge under the concrete paradise of a freeway overpass. It was populated by dozens of vagrants set up in hovels of all make and material. As I felt out a spot of my own, a large, dirty man approached me and began to mumble through his rotten teeth about how his blonde cock was just for his girlfriend. I was too afraid to say anything in response, and so I just kept my eyes on his feet, which were covered by a couple of bulky, homemade shoes. They were a massive conglomeration of toilet paper, cardboard, and duct tape, which covered his entire foot with the exception of a few dirty toes. He continued to talk about how I couldn't have his blonde cock, and I continued to ignore him. I began to worry that this was going to turn into a real confrontation, but he soon walked away and I could hear him spouting the same vulgarities to his dirty peers.

As I settled in for the night, my mind drifted to Jude's envelope while I kept my eye on the itinerants and squatters in their cardboard village who occupied the under-bridge with me. I was initially worried that I was entering a community that would immediately recognize as an outsider, but they were indifferent to me—each of them huddled or wandering in their ragged clothes, talking mostly to themselves, and honoring some demarcations of their needy suburb that I could not follow. I felt like I was watching those anthills from my childhood again, before I blew them up. The way they'd move in paths that seemed chaotic until you realized that every one of them knew exactly what it wanted to do, how it was going to do it, without ever stumbling over one of its associates.

I thought it was poetic. I figured it was time for me to go on my own path that, to an onlooker, would seem like chaos, but to me would be perfectly purposeful. It was time for me to be rid of the albatross that now hung very literally around my neck and be lightened of its burden. I'd take Jude's letter to where it belonged.

Sitting on a concrete incline, I opened the large manila envelope to mild disappointment. The months I had spent carrying it around had set within me some idea that it contained more than was reasonable. I considered the possibility that it contained a narrative of Jude's unbeknownst to anyone at that point—a final cleansing and unburdening of his hidden soul. Maybe it held some admission about Jude's history that he was not all that he had said he was—that he had absconded in the night with some other All-American boy's identity, claimed it as his own, and began to live up to ideals never available to him before in his unfortunate state. Maybe it would contain a picture of him with some overseas royal family and I would learn that Jude was the prince of said royal bloodline, that he fled to America to fight for higher ideals not held by his own country, and that I would be taken care of by his family for being such a close friend to him. I even dared to imagine a jump-drive that contained a video confession of Jude vocalizing all that he had been and all that he ever wanted to be. Instead, all I found were two more, smaller envelopes and a single key attached to a thin plastic, blue diamond shaped key chain that had the faded white letters of *Jones Brothers Realtors*. One envelope had my name written on the outside, the other the name of his wife. I sat there for a minute and looked at both.

Memphis was muggy that time of year and the letter entitled to me made no noise in my clammy grip. It was short. The letter's contents had the address of his wife, and instructed me to get the other letter to her in the case of his demise—he said mailing it to her would be fine, and would save me from the cost of delivering it in person. The key, he wrote, was for me. It would grant me access to a storage shed from the same town where his wife now lived, and contained artifacts from Jude's bachelor days that didn't make it into his and his wife's house after their marriage. He wrote that nothing in the shed would be of interest to her, and that I was free to whatever was of interest to me. He thanked me for being a friend to him, and that was it.

The key was a nice memento, but my half of Jude's gift left me with little satisfaction. The thick black-marker ink that identified the other one to *Vera* was etched into my eyes and mind, though I kept them away from the letter and on the cardboard ghetto below me. I felt like a dirty and malnourished angel looking down on the camp, but knew that my actions in minutes to come would make me something more of a demon. I don't know how long I sat there trying to talk myself out of it, but I think now that my mind was made from the moment I opened the larger envelope. I snatched her letter from the pack at my side, and my heart raced even more when I noticed it contained slightly more bulk than the one addressed to me. To calm myself I grabbed my gear and moved to the bottom of the incline and huddled between the slanted wall and a large concrete pillar that supported the highway above me where the citizens of Memphis still occasionally passed overhead on their way to wherever it is they flee when the sun goes down.

Finding a replacement for the envelope didn't concern me at all, and as I ran my hand across its surface to break the seal, I could feel the guilt cutting at my fingers. I peeked inside to find, again, only a letter, but this one measuring nearly four lined-pages of paper in Jude's clean handwriting. I bit a small flashlight into my teeth and pointed it at the letter that I now gripped in front of me with two hands that I rested on my pulled up knees. The dusk sun, the sound of traffic retreated against my focus, and the artificial glow of flashlight reflected the black ink back at my desperate eyes.

Vera,

If you are reading this then my worst nightmare has become a reality. I'm so sorry, baby. I'd like to tell you that I never could've imagined this would happen, but the existence of this letter is proof that I have indeed considered the worst. I think I wasn't able to fully consider this outcome because of you, Vera. Before leaving, I couldn't imagine being without you and I couldn't imagine the pain I would put you through if I couldn't return. I feel the need to try to fit within this letter every feeling I've ever had for you, but I know that I cannot, and I take solace in knowing that that's what our time together was for, and not the purpose of this letter. The question that continually runs through my mind, and the impetus for these final words, is that if I was certain I was going to die would I still have enlisted last year? It's not an easy question because of what this has done to you, but let me try to justify myself now in a way that I could not put to words before I left.

I consider myself lucky to have gotten the time and clarity needed for a decision like the one I made. So often life altering decisions are thrust upon people in demanding and adverse times, thus potentially putting such a decision at risk. Other times people are unaware that such a decision is at hand, and they haphazardly choose one result, unaware that so many factors hinge on that decision. I was fortunate enough to recognize this decision for what it was and weigh it appropriately. You were, of course, a major factor in my choice to enlist, but I must be honest when I admit that I knew, intuitively, at the moment of its conception. I could hear a voice leading me to this moment. I imagine that voice is the version of myself that I most want to become—the best version of me—and it told me that this was the path I had to walk to become that person. I wanted to become that person for me, yes, but I also wanted to become that person for you, for our family, and for the world at large.

None of this is to say that I was at all unhappy. It is my belief that I could have continued selling insurance and coaching youth baseball, and you could have kept teaching, and we could have carved out a nice life for ourselves—really, a remarkable one by most standards. The day I married you was the happiest one of my life, and I had no reason but to suspect many more of those days—the days our own children would be born, the days of their accomplishments, and the days when they had marriages and children of their own.

Life was good, but it was not enough. I can hear my own selfishness in that last sentence, but I cannot help that it is the truth. I've spent my life pursuing excellence in many walks of life. The pursuit of that excellence led to numerous athletic accomplishments, a college degree, and a crossing of paths with fascinating peers, coaches, and, of course, you. However, the attacks on our country—our home where our kids would one day grow up—made me realize just how shallow and insignificant my role was. I believed that the decision I made would walk hand in hand with sacrifice and adversity, but I also believed that pursuing that voice would make both our lives, and the lives of our future family, fuller and more meaningful.

So would I have enlisted last year knowing that it would come to this? We both know that I would have, and I tell myself that that is why you love me so much. If I hadn't enlisted, then that version of me would have forever been a ghost. I would've had to spend the rest of my days knowing that I could've been better for you and for our kids, if only I had been courageous enough to pursue myself into a distant desert.

Even though I've written a piece of my heart into this letter, I pray that you never have to read it. But know that if you are, that I am reading it with you—that my heart is breaking with yours, and that the hatred I feel for myself in hurting you like this is only outweighed by the certainty that what I did was the right thing to do. As I write, I hope that these are not my last words to you, but if they are, I hope that they have brought comfort to you in some way. Good bye, Love.

Forever Yours,
Jude

The North Star

The veterinary clinic was a square, flat-roofed building located just outside of the city's limits. Silvio stood out back in the outside pens where he used the water from a garden hose to push dirt and feces off of the pen's concrete foundations. At the base of the building's brick exterior grew a deep green vine that climbed up portions of the building's side as if one stretch of bricks was easier to scale than others. He studied its pattern and challenged himself to find some logic to the vine's growth but he deduced nothing and was eventually entranced by the quicksilver visual of the hose's water as it slithered over the concrete pallets. When he was done he rolled the hose onto a plastic wheel that was drilled into the building's side and slipped into the back door. He was met by a middle-aged woman in a white overcoat and she said to him, I heard you were looking for me.

Silvio said, I was wondering who's on death row today.

We don't call it that.

Whatever you call it. Who's on it?

The veterinary assistant used a nod of her head to gesture him to follow. They walked down two hallways that were lined from the floor to the ceiling with stacked cells that held the lethargic bodies of dogs and cats. Some dogs summoned the energy to bark at the two as they passed and Silvio glanced in curiously at a small mixed-breed whose lonely head peered out from inside a large plastic cone. In a back room, under a dim lightbulb, they peered into a crate that held the shaggy form of a cat. There was a slip of paper above the crate's door.

Silvio said, Its name is Dirtbag?

And she said, Affectionately so.

Silvio wedged a finger through the crate's metal door and attempted to entice the cat over to him. It lifted its head and he saw that its left eye was missing and crusted over with scar tissue. Its hair was several shades of dirty gray, and it was long and knotted. He puckered his lips and the cat waved its tail. The tail was unnaturally short and when he asked her what happened to it, she didn't say anything. The cat wouldn't approach him and he withdrew his hand from the crate.

She said, It's an ugly cat.

Silvio said, I know it is. I'm looking at it.

And you want her?

How much for a neuter?

You mean a spay?

Yeah.

I can't remember. Like a hundred bucks maybe.

How long does that take?

She shrugged her shoulders.

He said, I'll take it.

Later that night, Silvio stood in an open dirt field south of town that was once used for agriculture but hadn't been worked for untold years. In the neighboring acres were erected row upon row of mature corn stalks that basked in the dusk light not unlike him that stood there. Around him were men and women of varying ages, all wearing the same Fire Department shirt that Silvio did, moving about aimlessly now that everything for the firework show was prepared. All that needed to be set now was the sun, and this Silvio watched from the field as it slowly sank like a ship into the sparse vegetation and white rock of the valley lip. He didn't move a muscle as the skyline faded through all its brilliant renditions of red, and finally dissolved into black. He remained unmoved as the absence of one light revealed the presence of a thousand others. He kept his eyes there and no attention was paid by him to the fireworks that crashed into the black canvas above in all their spectacle of red and white and blue. When the final barrage knocked the wind from his lungs he stood unmoved and, with his peers, packed away the launch equipment. A couple of the younger men in the department invited him out for beers, but he politely declined and started his walk home.

The next afternoon found him in one of the city's small parks, sitting alongside the old man on one of the park's few benches with a cheeseburger, bratwurst, and pile of potato chips heaped onto a paper plate. He received dozens of thanks and compliments for doing the grilling, but he only deflected the compliments to other congregation members. When the party thinned out, only the old man was left beside him, watching some of the younger park-goers from the neighboring gazebo throw around a football and hearing occasional cheers from the nearby ballpark. Silvio told the old man that he had met another volunteer at the library.

A girl?

A woman.

They're all girls when you get to my age.

Silvio rolled his eyes.

Married?

How should I know?

They tend to wear rings when they're married.

The kids they were watching had given up on all semblance of order and resorted to gang tackling whichever one was brave enough to pick the ball up, until that one fumbled the ball to the next audacious child. Their energy was relentless and they were rejuvenated every time one of the baseball-induced cheers from the distance happened to coincide with any of their efforts. On and on they went. And most remarkable to Silvio was that even in the intense heat of the sun directly overhead, they appeared never to sweat, never to fatigue. He wondered where in their tiny bodies they stored all of that energy and he wondered where it had gone inside of himself. He looked at the damaged skin of the old man that acted as a hide against the heat.

Silvio said, She lives right across the street from the church. She said she had seen me before, walking there.

You should have invited her to the cookout.

I did.

Then you should invite her over to the church sometime.

I did.

And?

Silvio shrugged. He finished the last of the food on his plate and walked it to a nearby receptacle where the mob of determined youths nearly took him out at the knees. A distant aluminum clink brought another round of cheers to Silvio's ears as he retook his seat on the bench.

Silvio wiped his hands on the thighs of his jeans as he said, You know what I was thinking about last night?

I can't imagine.

The North Star.

Is that right?

Yeah, Silvio said.

What about it?

As Silvio talked, he tried to use his hands in big rotating gestures to make his point. He said, I was thinking. . .we're here in space, and we are rotating around this fixed spot, and out here are all of these stars and planets—and we can see them. And, so it makes sense, that depending on where we are at in our rotation, we see different things out there. Different constellations are seen best at different times of the year. And that makes sense to me.

That makes sense to me too.

But the North Star doesn't make sense to me.

Why not?

Well, because it doesn't move like the rest. It's more constant, but how can that be? How can something like that star never seem to move in a universe where nothing is static? It's impressive to me, that star. But I don't get it.

The old man crumpled a pleated napkin and set it on his plate with the uneaten remnants of his meal. He then brushed the fingertips of his pointer and middle finger across the corners of his lip. He said, I've never really thought about it, but I'm sure there is a good and reasonable explanation as to why that star is so special.

I'm sure there is too.

I wish I could help you out Silvio, but I'm not a cosmologist.

I know that.

My turn.

For what?

A question.

Shoot.

If you really tried, you know that you could find the answer to your question in a matter of minutes—so why don't you?

Silvio wiped his hands on his jeans again. The improvised game of football had died down as each of the kids' parents had begun to leave the park until one was left, attempting to catch the ball after kicking it as high into the air as she could. Sounds from the baseball games could still be heard but at least one of the games must have ended, as a convoy of vehicles rolled by the park from the direction of the fields. Silvio recognized one of the vehicles and offered an unenthusiastic wave of his hand before he said,

I don't know. Sometimes I just like wondering more than I like knowing.

Silvio Submission Six:

DEATH OF THE SUNSET

It has grown self-conscious
through the years—
the endless interpretations of artists,
the optimistic gaze of young lovers,
peeking over the counter of the
Earth's crust.

Crudely sketched on a cave wall
with a nearby fire in its braggart form.

Now it rises over the pale crest of the
Earth to find, yet again,
that tireless painter with all his hues
of red at the ready, and
the eager poet armed with his pen
and his adjectives—

to find the shaman with his bloody dagger who
has once again failed to appease the angry god.

Vera

Being predated by older siblings in a small community was her beast of burden. Sometimes, having one of your kind go before you can act as a blessing of sorts—teachers are charmed by the living versions of their past ghosts, peers are eager to befriend someone with access to the wisdom and resources of more mature associations, the runts themselves are hardened and made wise by their constant presence on the bottom of their respective totem pole, and the opportunity to learn from mistakes not their own. The latter was her only benefit, and so Vera spent her adolescence in the standard misery of being a small-town youth, compounded by the constant preoccupation with how to escape both.

Her oldest sister, Olivia, never made it out of high school. She developed early, physically, in the months after their dad walked out, and basked in the mostly harmless ogling of the junior high boys around her. Upon graduating to high school, she graduated to the more graphic and unintentionally bawdy advancements of upper classmen, to which she often acquiesced. She'd smoke pot with them and have sex with them and go to parties in dirt fields where the only light came from the headlights of cars and the older girls openly resented her for getting the attention from the boys they also desired but weren't willing to earn the way she did. And the girls from her own class hated her for the same reason. Six months prior to receiving her diploma, she turned eighteen years old, dropped out of high school, and moved into her thirty-five-year-old boyfriend's trailer house. Vera never talked to her, or her to Vera, and rumors of her sister's heavy drug use reached her twelve-year-old ears. Over winter break of Vera's eighth grade year, Olivia visited home, very pregnant, to fight with their mother one last time before saying goodbye. Olivia's boyfriend had been sentenced to time in a penitentiary for drug distribution and Olivia was moving to be closer to him during his incarceration. She didn't say a word to Vera before she left.

Her next oldest sister, Lucille, was sixteen and a sophomore in high school at this time. She took the predictable flak from her peers in regards to her promiscuous sister who dropped out only half a year before graduating, and when she found no comfort in the sunken eyes of her mother, she put her emotional investment into the first serious boyfriend to come along. His name was Tom, and within four and a half months of Olivia absconding from their small town, Lucille too was pregnant. Values prevented her from aborting the pregnancy, and her secret desire to wrangle Tom into a marriage veiled any discussion of adoption into a moralistic stance from Lucille. When Vera registered for freshman classes in the Fall, her would-be-Junior-sister was seven months pregnant and enrolled in an online GED program. Tom had dropped out and left town to work in some distant oil field. He and Lucille didn't talk.

Having what she deemed to be a damning and embarrassing familial legacy, Vera adopted her mother's maiden name and took to something neither her parents or sisters had ever shown any interest in—athletics. The name change did little to protect her identity in a community so small, but her previously undiscovered athletic prowess allowed her to carve out a more complicated one in the eyes of others. She shone as a point guard in the winter and as a long distance runner in the spring, but in the fall, during the volleyball season, was where she made a name for herself. As a sophomore she was contributing to matches as the starting setter and returning home to babysit Lucille's daughter while she was out on dates with men she wasn't entirely interested in but were effective at fragmenting the mundane life of single motherhood that she never wanted and never could get rid of.

In the fall of Vera's junior year, word came that Olivia had moved east with a new boyfriend, freshly released from incarceration. She had her second child in tow. Lucille was still single and worked as a bank teller where nearly half of her monthly paycheck went to daycare for Alex—her daughter—whose father was still working one-week-on, one-week-off shifts in the oil fields to pay for his new-model pickup truck. He had also taken up a nasty drinking habit and skimping on his monthly child-support paycheck, arbitrarily deciding that Alex was not his and that he had no duty to raise and support such a child. When threatened with legal action, the checks again came monthly. Vera was All-State in both volleyball and basketball.

She had a slew of wannabe suitors, but by the time she was a senior, she had established for herself such a reputation among her peers that the boys in the class didn't bother to even flirt with her anymore. She continued to babysit Alex on the weekends while her mom watched cable movies and Lucille used her new job as the receptionist at a local law firm to network dates and a night life with the clients that were in need of an attorney. Drunk drivers, low-grade drug dealers, assault and battery offenders—real winners, all of them. Before the volleyball season was even over, Vera accepted a scholarship to play for the state university the following fall. The two-hundred-seventeen miles between her town and the university was purgatory for her, and it marked a distance from home that was further than she had ever been before. Olivia was in the wind—still out east as far as any of them knew. Lucille couldn't wait to use Vera as an excuse to visit a city with an excess of what she deemed to be young, handsome, educated, and privileged men. In her head she was already working on approaches and strategies to telling the bachelors about her daughter back home. Mom continued to fill her emptiness with fictional movies that were based on true stories in all the ways that weren't actually important to the stories being told. None of them knew it, but their father was now dead—buried alive with a handful of other men in a coal mine in West Virginia. The daughters never knew why he left in the first place.

Her first year at university wasn't a fulfillment of all her city dreams more than it was an escape from her small town nightmares. She tolerated dorm life and cafeteria food and, though many of her classmates had also moved on to the same college, she, for the first time, felt the freedom to establish an unencumbered identity. However, the freedom was short lived due to her position on the volleyball team, and it didn't take long for her conditioning workouts and practices and team meetings and diet and study sessions and perpetual ponytail and sweatpants to isolate her from the other students on her floor. Her teammates were supportive and attempted to be sister-like to her, but either her past experience with sisters or her own limitations prevented the growth of any real bonds. Most of them were preoccupied with boyfriends of their own, and the ones that were of age would frequent the local clubs and the ones that weren't of age would frequent the same clubs anyway. Vera didn't care much for the atmosphere of the clubs or bars and so she spent most of her weekends hallowed out in her dorm room with her undeclared and apathetic roommate who spent hour after hour watching bad television dramas and movies. Vera resented her. Lucille would call once a week behind the veil of *staying in touch*, but was only biding her time for when Vera's roommate would leave town for a weekend and she could finally visit.

She met Jude in the fall of her sophomore year but paid him little attention. By this time she had settled into an elementary education major and one of Jude's teammates and friends, Christopher, shared many classes with her. The romantic limitations of her past became a detriment to her interest in Christopher when she could not decide on the appropriate way to show her feelings. They would talk and she couldn't help but laugh at his jokes that weren't really funny and show a supreme fascination in all of his ideas and thoughts. When he and Jude would talk to her at the gym, her focus was on Christopher, Jude's was on her, and Christopher's was elsewhere entirely. Her teammates were constantly on about how cute Jude was and how smart he was and how he came from a good family and how he had a nice posterior and how he was perfect for Vera. None of the boyfriends of the other players showed up to as many matches as Jude did, and he hadn't gotten so much as a date. He was engaged in her matches from beginning to end and when they were over he would mingle outside the locker room until she came out so he could rehash her most outstanding plays of the evening. She was flattered but indifferent to his flirtations and polite enough to ask generic questions of her own about how baseball and school was going for him. Baseball was going well, school was going well, and so on. He was majoring in agriculture, minoring in biology, and so on. His family owned a ranch, he had two sisters of his own, and so on. When the volleyball season was over he continued to talk to her whenever he saw her around campus, and when she returned home over winter break and made some money waitressing at the same truck stop that Lucille now worked at, Jude continued making occasional phone calls driven by small talk and trifling sessions of question and answer. In the spring he began inviting her to watch his baseball games and she consented out of a combination of her boredom, her continued interest in Christopher, and her inability to decline any of Jude's advancements without feeling a sense of rudeness and guilt.

After a summer break consumed by the truck stop and babysitting and weekly updates from Jude, who was working on the family ranch back in his own home town, Vera was invited to end the summer by spending a weekend at the lake house of one of her teammates. And three days before returning to training and practice, she tore the ACL ligament of her right knee while waterskiing for the first time in her life. Her return to campus was made worse by her new roommate assignment, a freshman teammate who would now be replacing her as the starting setter. The endless and pointless cable stories of her old roommate were replaced by optimism and energy of the same type. Bound to her wheelchair and then her crutches, she watched as what she had rightfully earned was given away to someone else, and she had to endure the continual presence of the person who took it. However, she was fortunate enough to retain her scholarship through the course of her junior year, but was informed at the end of the season that they would be rescinding it at the conclusion of the spring semester—her freshman counterpart was playing well and, given the uncertainty of her recovery, the team thought it best to open her roster spot for a younger athlete. *To build the program*, they said.

Jude was at her perpetual behest. He took care of all the simple errands made difficult by her injury and lent a listening ear to her struggles. She could go to his apartment anytime she needed to escape her roommate or cafeteria food and he would willingly cook up a meal and listen to any of the doubts and adversities she now faced. She spent many a day there. Christopher was one of his three roommates. By the time Vera returned home for another summer of truck-stopping, Lucille had moved into her latest boyfriend's house, a bank teller, and Olivia had returned from her sabbatical back east, boyfriend-less and with another child in her custody—they all lived at home, with mom. Vera tired of the babysitting routine and Olivia's mocking questions as to why Vera worked as a waitress if she was in college, and why she could no longer play volleyball, and why they had given her scholarship away, and how much money was she going to make as a teacher, and why she just couldn't be a lawyer or an engineer or something that made more money, and if the guy she was dating was going to make a lot of money or was he just a teacher or something too. To escape, she made the eight-hour round trip to Jude's hometown anytime she had more than two consecutive days off. Vera quickly gathered that Jude was raised to play baseball. The men in his family had been good at baseball for almost as long as they had settled the family ranch and Jude was to be no exception. He had two older sisters but Vera never met either of them—they had played softball for each of their respective colleges and moved away the minute they graduated. Athletics was no means to an education, and quite the opposite was true. Jude was good, but not big leagues good. And so he would inherit the ranch. She declined his first marriage proposal at the end of the summer, certain that she could not spend her life on that *desolate ranch*. And, when he agreed, she declined his second proposal one week later, certain that if he were to try to make it on the minor league baseball circuit that she would not be happy with how often he would travel. They talked for two more weeks, and when he agreed that he would do neither of those, she accepted his proposal on the grass of the university's quad.

She was now determined to leave the university behind just as far as she did her hometown, and he was ostracized—some rotten damsel taking him away from the entire of what he was raised to be. Wedded in a courthouse. Honeymooned in a small town out west that they decided to take as their home when she was hired on to teach second grade. Two years of financially establishing themselves before having children. Sixteen months of American happiness until the consumption to go to war was born inside Jude before a baby was in her.

I continued making my way, by foot, north on 55. I thought that walking at night was too suspicious and would bring unwanted attention my way, and so I kept my travels to the daytime where it was common for me to see a handful of individuals who looked a lot like me. I was continually tempted by the smells that came out of the area's many barbeque shacks. However, I stayed disciplined and bypassed them all, because all it took was one misgiving business owner and I'd be rounded up by the authorities in no time. I stuck to a steady diet of bread and peanut butter because it was filling, it stored easy in my pack, and it was readily available in every convenient store along the highway.

I spent my nights wherever I could find a hiding place—roadside foliage, bridge underpasses, and in the high weeds around neglected commercial property. Near the end of the fifth day, as I began scouting out a spot for the night, I was startled by the quick horn of a semi truck and the driver's offer for a ride. He must have been in his early thirties and we didn't say much other than some quick small talk. I appreciated that he was willing to just let me be, because I was content to stare out the dirty passenger window and let my feet rest. Occasionally, the Mississippi river would snake into view and, as I admired the moonlight on its shaking surface, I realized that this was the first time I had taken the river into thought even though it had shadowed my every step since Jackson. One of the world's great rivers sliding unnoticed through my peripheral. But not anymore.

Anytime I saw or heard about the Mississippi river I inevitably was drawn back to my junior year in high school, where we were required to read *Huckleberry Finn*. I don't remember much about that book other than the entire class period my teacher spent ranting on how great the part is when Huck decides that he would rather go to hell than betray his friend

Jim back into slavery. I guess I thought it was a pretty cool move by Huck, but I don't think I believed in Hell at the time and I never had a great friend like Jim was to Huck, so maybe a lot of the significance was lost on me. But, looking out from the cab of that truck onto the glass surface of the Mississippi, I revisited in my mind the time Huck decided he might just go to hell. It didn't matter if *I* believed in hell or not—Huck believed in Hell, and he was the one doing the deciding. He weighed in one hand all that he had been raised to think and believe about Jim's place in the world, and he tried to pray for forgiveness from the Almighty for helping with Jim's escape because he was raised to believe he was doing the wrong thing. And he couldn't do it. For the life of him he couldn't pray, because he *knew* it wasn't wrong. Sometimes it just happens that way. Parents and teachers and preachers and politicians and friends and grandparents and cousins and the whole world can tell you that something is the way it is, and you *know*—you know deep down inside you in some place that you didn't know existed until you had no other choice but to discover it—you *know* that you can't listen to them. That old lady that raised Huck? She would have said the prayer and she would have felt it through and through. It would have been right for *her* in a way that it never could be for Huck.

I thought about the day I walked off the base and went AWOL. I tried to talk myself out of it, and I tried to make myself feel the guilt as heavily as I could. And I genuinely missed the guys in my unit, but I knew that I wasn't equipped for one more day in the service. I knew from down in that place that I discovered that my desertion was my Huck moment. Everyone in the world could tell me it was the wrong thing to do, one way or the other, but I knew then at some level, and I know clearly now, that it was my moment where I decided to go to hell. I'm not saying I'm wired like the Huckleberry's of the world, but I like to think that he would have done exactly what I did if he had seen Jim leave the world the way that Jude did. Could you imagine some steamship rolling down the Mississippi river and blasting Jim to smithereens from the very ship that Huck sat on? I bet readers would just go ahead and leave *Huckleberry Finn* on the shelf. There wouldn't be any book clubs for a story like that. Twain could've changed the face of American literature by turning a cannon to Jim, but why on Earth would he want to do that? Who would want to enter into a world where soft hearted slave runaways get mindlessly and violently annihilated? Nobody, is who. If they can't handle the n-word, then they sure won't know how to manage the death of Jim. I sure didn't.

We entered into southern St. Louis later that night and I thanked the stoic driver. I felt energized by the small amount of time I got to get off of my feet and out of the sun. I moved through the streets of St. Louis as clandestine as I did Memphis, and with the extra week of wear I had put onto myself and my clothes, it was effortless for me now to appear as just another moldy itinerant. Like Memphis, I found a hedge-covered sleep in a park for a few nights and a place next to the Missouri river after that. I stayed next to the river for nearly a week, resting, eating, and deciding how best to proceed to my destination. I'd eventually have to head far west, and because the Missouri river cut that very direction, I decided to shadow it much like I had the Mississippi. It was about as good of a route as any, and it allowed me to stick with the interstate, which had given me great fortune in terms of hitchhiking and being left alone, thus far.

The next morning, I began my journey out of St. Louis along interstate 70. For the next three days the world spun me into the west and into that which waited for me there. On the fourth morning, I realized that traveling the country west of the Mississippi was like visiting an entirely different planet. By the next afternoon, after only a few dozen miles of walking, the earth flattened out so much that everything other than the corn became inconsequential. So flat. I felt that at any moment I might trip and accidentally fall into space. That night, as I slept a stone's throw away from a rest stop in the one acre of the state not covered with corn, I looked off the edge of the Earth. The land around and ahead of me was so flat that I could see the very line where the stars above met the darkness ahead. Not even the desert overseas had a horizon like that.

The next evening, row after row of corn dominated my eyes as I looked out from, for the first time in my journey, the inside of somebody's car. She was a student at the University of Kansas and was on her way back from Louisville to get ready for the fall semester. She said she had never picked up a hitchhiker before but that I looked harmless enough and that she had grown tired of her book on tape. She was a graduate student in Agriculture, and we talked at length about what she studied specifically, I just can't recall any of it. When the conversation turned to me I figured was best to tell as much of the truth as possible, because I wasn't much of a liar and I didn't trust myself enough to tell a convincing one. The last thing I wanted to do was to raise any suspicions about myself. I said that I was a serviceman, and after a full tour in Iraq, I had left the service. I could feel her measuring me up out of the side of her eye at hearing that I was a soldier, but I felt no hostility from her as the sun began to set. After a few minutes of silence she said that she thought that it was too bad what sometimes happens with soldiers. She related to me a story of a man from her hometown who was just a year ahead of her in high school—a father of three. He was a marine and among the first waves of units sent to Iraq. She didn't know specifics, just that when he was done with his tour he returned home with stories of IED's and mass graves. His family was worried at first but he settled back into normalcy and after a few months he seemed like the husband and father of old. Not long after that, he drove alone to a popular camping site in the area, sat himself in the flames of a large bonfire he had made, and then took his own life with a pistol. Her final words lingered with the sound of the engine for several minutes, and then she apologized for telling me the story. She said it was probably best for stories like that one not to be told. I said it was fine.

When the lights of Kansas City began to mirror the stars overhead, I tried to say the first genuine prayer of my life from the passenger seat of that girl's car. I could hardly remember how it worked—about formalities I should take—but I thought real intently about the man who took his own life and about his family, and I thought about Jude. I thought I didn't know where they were or who was taking care of them, but I hoped they were all right. To whoever was listening, I said that those men had been through more than any man should be asked to go, and that they deserved some real peace. I prayed that their families found that peace too. When I parted ways with the young woman at a truck stop, I walked out past where all the semi-trailers hauled in for the night, and I wept. How long did I have before I was willing to baptize myself by fire? I wept for the man and for Jude and for their families, and for the fear that whatever lay dormant inside that man for those few months might be crouched in me now. I wept for Huckleberry Finn and the image of him lighting out for the territories at the end of the novel—maybe when he declared his resignation to go to Hell he got exactly what was coming to him.

Service

He gave what he knew how to give. There was not a function or a chore that went beyond his notice, and he became a popular and sought out staple among the members of the congregation. As the priest took handshakes and questions in regards to his sermon, Silvio took an even greater number of the same about his writing and his availability for service. He became a forced dabbler in plumbing, carpentry, landscaping, cooking, and any other craft he needed to when service called. Nearly every day of the week called upon him to be somewhere to help a congregation member in need. He mended leaks, freed sticky door jambs, cleared clogged drains, mowed lawns, trimmed hedges, fixed broken chair legs, fixed broken table legs, tightened loose sink handles, tightened toilet interiors, painted fences, painted houses, painted trim, shingled roofs, re-shingled roofs, dug post holes, poured concrete, attached rain gutters, re-attached rain gutters—he attended and assisted every event the church had to offer, and he wrote.

In mid-July he received approval to do some mild renovations to the church grounds, and he decided to add a flower garden on the backside of the building's lawn. He sought to charm with humbleness and simplicity. He removed a thirty-square-foot semi-circle of sod tucked against the brick wall of the building and lined the edge of the torn out lawn with a narrow and matching brick path. From there he added another section to the path that split the semi-circle in half and met the church at the base of the building, where Silvio planted a white decorative pedestal with nothing on it. He told people he was looking for the perfect statue to place upon it. From there, he filled in around the path with good soil and filled in each side with varying colors of gaillardias, geraniums, dahlias, and creeping thyme—all accentuated by yellow day lilies. Some of the congregation joked that he was a little late in the season to be planting a garden, but they adored its addition to the property and voiced opinions about other possible changes.

After two more conversations in the shelves of the public library, he convinced Vera to join him on a service call. He mowed the lawn for a man too elderly to do so himself, and she managed the trimming. All the while she maintained her propensity for silence and chain smoking, and he respected her reserve. He noticed her ring and asked if she was married. She pretended to not hear the question and he didn't ask it again. The following Monday he convinced her to call numbers at the weekly bingo while he ran the concessions stand, and he got her to travel to the state diocese with a van load of the congregation where they held two candlelight vigils in front of abortion clinics. She told him that she took no issue with abortion and he told her that there was nothing wrong with that. The vigils were to pray for the dead souls, not condemn the live ones.

On the trip home from the vigil, as the large van traversed a long stretch of dark highway, the two of them sat alone in the last row—all asleep but the driver. Her head rested on the cool window as she gazed out at the passing blackness, and he sat with his knees tucked near his chest and propped on the back of the seat ahead of him, looking ahead into the dim yellow shadows of the van's headlights. She admitted to him that she had never gone to church as a child—it didn't appeal to her then and it didn't now. She claimed to tag along now only to combat her loneliness—because she had nothing better to do. She used to be a teacher at the town's elementary school, but resigned after being charged with the drunk driving offense.

What to do now? He noticed that she no longer had the ring on the appropriate finger, and she talked about the office job she had taken doing data-entry and budget balancing. She was a part time laborer with no husband and a pariah in the field of her profession that she had gone to four years of college for. She told Silvio that maybe this was the price she had to pay for her sins. Twenty-three years of spiritual indifference come home to roost. And then she said that she didn't want to hear anything about it being a test either. She didn't want to hear that this was all God's way of finding out what she was made of. She had already had her test. She failed. This was the retribution. She had ignored the god and now it was going to do anything but.

Silvio looked at the grim profile of her face leaning against the window, and then took measure of the dangled and sleeping heads of the people in the van. When he began talking, he leaned his head near her ear as she continued to look out into the night. He said that he thought God to be the Alpha and the Omega—the beginning and the middle and the end to everything that ever has been and will be. Everything that *is* can only be so with his knowledge and his consent, because how else could it be for a creator of his pedigree? Some may point to the Devil as a perversion to that creation, but he is only a proxy to God's power—another essence that exists only because he allows it to. You think there could be perversion in his world if he didn't have in him the ability to create such a thing? It's all him. There is no indifference to the omniscient and omnipresent—you could live your life indifferent to the atom, but that wouldn't change the fact that it molds you and the entire world around you. You never hurt his feelings and you never affronted him, because you couldn't. There was nothing you did that he didn't allow you to do. You could go worship trees, rocks, people, other gods, but no matter. They are all him because what else could they be? And someone who wants to worship something other than God can sure try, but there is no other entity to be paid homage. He's a black hole of grace to which we're all doomed. Don't fret that your past wasn't filled with Matthew and Mark and Luke and John, because they are no more privileged than Shakespeare and Dante and Tolstoy and Faulkner. What does the Bible have that they don't? The word of God? All words are that of God. All of them. Some are just better vessels for delivering them than others, and some men who you would never associate with a religion are the best vessels there are. There is no difference between prophets and those that masquerade as them, and you know why. Don't demarcate yourself from him, or him from the world. He will forgive your indifference because there is no such thing in regard to him. And he will forgive your sin because he's the one who created that sin, and you in the midst of it. You can hold onto the belief that there is one way to recognize God and that you have failed to do so thus far, but I'm telling you that there are an infinite number of ways to recognize him, and the more ways we do, the closer to him we'll be. Don't cage him into one church or one sect or one book or one vision, because one or two or a dozen of any of those things simply isn't adequate. He *is* salvation and happiness and grace, but he is pain and anger and tragedy all the same.

Silvio stopped when a young man in the bench ahead of him began to stir. When he was sure that the dreamer had returned, he continued. He said, I spent a lot of my life up to his point worrying about what God thought of me, and I'm not sure I ever considered what I thought of him.

It felt blasphemous and pointless to consider the nature of his *being* rather than simply accept the fact of his existence. Maybe if you do that—consider what you think of him. . .maybe that can help you.

He wasn't sure if she was still listening, or if she ever was, and so he returned his attention back to the hazy amber highway lighted before him. He thought that over the passing of the tires on the asphalt below him he could hear her teeth grinding within her skull, which still pressed against the window pane. Outside passed the night and within it the shadowy figures of antelope and deer that either spooked at the clamor of the vehicle or calibrated its passing with the slow turn of their necks—the headlights drawing a faint glow upon every iris. Minutes later when she first spoke, Silvio could only hear her mumble underneath her breath to those extraneous ghosts. When he asked for his pardon, she turned to him and whispered,

I think I hate him.

Silvio Submission Seven:

MOTHER

I wonder if Jesus ever felt
the inadequacy of thanking his mother
for all the things that a mother
can never be thanked for—
or was she just another sheep in the flock?

Did she feel the same about
her God-son, who can hardly
be thanked for his own intangible deeds?

Did she cry in the sparse
vegetation of that hill as a disciple,
or as a mother witnessing the slow
death of her miraculous child?

Flesh of her flesh,
blood of her blood—
I've only loved gods as gods
and sons as sons.

I'd never seen anything in my entire life like that cloud. I was five days west of Kansas City, where I spent some time off of my feet and getting my supplies straight. As the city began to thin out, I lurked off to the side of highway 70 for a snack of bread and peanut butter when I first noticed it. At first, it appeared ordinary enough—a white cloud front that, from my position, didn't seem to be moving anywhere fast. But after few more hours of walking west, as it crept over my position like an immeasurable spaceship, I realized it to be a different beast altogether. Its white exterior built itself endlessly upward into the atmosphere, and below was cast its thick and moving shadow. When it finally made its way over my head, I swear that for several minutes I thought the world was about to end. The density of the thing alone darkened a midsummer afternoon into a concocted midnight. I wasn't sure what to do. Like anyone, I knew that this area of the country was notorious for its tornadoes, but I didn't know what happened in the moments leading up to a tornado, and began to think that maybe this was it. I wasn't so desperate to go knocking on some country house for shelter and risk getting barraged by questions and suspicions by a paranoid farmer, and so I looked for anything else to strand myself within. In the flatness of that country, in an open field, I chose a scantily, wooden framed windmill for which to lie in wait—it was my only option. There I huddled and admired the mid-eve nighttime that soon enveloped me. Promptly after the faux darkness settled in, so too did the steady murmur of thunder. Next came the rain, and though I've been in torrential rain several times before, I've never again seen lightning like that. When it began to spark and branch from the black island above, I measured the rapidly spinning windmill fan above me and decided not to worry too much over its conductivity. Its metal fan was a beacon for electrical attraction, but the little protection the wooden slats gave me from the wind and the rain was worth any risk of a lightning strike. Strangely enough, the thought of getting toasted by a bit of lightning didn't bother me a bit. I figured when I was enlisted and shipping off overseas that I was asking for it—I was putting myself in a position to be killed. In that chaos, things that aren't meant to happen, happen. But, if I were struck down by lightning in the middle of Kansas beneath an old windmill in the heart of some thunderstorm that I never could have previously imagined, well then that's just meant to be. I wish I had felt the same way about going to war. I wish that I could go back to the days and weeks leading up to Iraq and change my view to something like the one I had of that storm—come to terms with the arbitrary and helpless nature of my fate. A helpless peace.

The lightning in that darkness was otherworldly, and I was awestruck by the display of it. Bolt after bolt struck at every square inch of the land around me, and it didn't stop there. Smaller bolts and their thousands of branches lit off continually within the clouds overhead just as often as they struck out toward the earth. For an indeterminate amount of time, all I could do was take in its profound expression. As I adjusted to the wonder around me, I realized that the lightning revealed no tornado barreling toward my position and, in fact, the wind became strangely calm. Having decided that my life was not immediately in danger, it occurred to me just how miserable I was under my windmill. I was soaked to my bones, and the ground I sat in had long ago turned to mud and was so saturated that it began to hold water above ground level. I didn't have any options as far as dealing with the discomfort, so I pulled my knees up to my chest and leaned up against a base-post of the windmill. After what must have been hours, I began to fall in and out of sleep. But it never came for more than several minutes at a time, and after a few failed attempts I tried to occupy my mind in the hopes of passing the night more quickly.

It was a surprise to me that the first thing that came to mind was my loneliness. Above all else—the desertion, Jude's death, my future, the apparent insanity of my every action since Jude's death—was the thought of me being pummeled by rain and lightning underneath a probably forgotten agricultural relic without a single soul on the face of the earth knowing about it. Again, I couldn't help but chuckle at the grim idea of being found dead somewhere out here. They'd eventually find out who I was, and you'd have to hire one hell of a storyteller to explain how it is I ended up being smote down in the middle of a part of the country I had never been within a thousand miles of in my entire life up to that point. Maybe I would become a useful piece of military and religious propaganda. *You see what happens when you abandon your brothers in arms? There's no hiding from God's judgment—not in Iraq, not in Kansas.* But there'd be no one to mourn me. My mother succumbed to multiple sclerosis a year before I enlisted and my dad's heart failed him at the age of fifty-one, just eight months later. I had no siblings and so it was up to me to carry on the family name, the family legacy—and what did I do? I signed up to get killed.

Early in enlistment, I could only admire the other young men around me and their attitudes of invincibility. Witnessing my mother's relatively slow degeneration and my father's cardiac arrest had forever changed my youthful notions of mortality. As my mom revved up her church visits and spiritual attitude in her final months, my dad distanced himself from it. She was comforted by it, and he resented that she was being taken away from him by the very thing she worshiped. I was caught somewhere in the middle—trying to be the support that each of them needed within their own ideas of the way things should be. After her death, my dad stopped going to church all together. He passed his Sunday mornings on our front porch looking at a lot of nothing. Cars and pedestrians would pass by and wave, but he'd never wave back. I don't even think he saw them. The funny thing with me is that I'm a born believer. I'm wired to be able to believe anything. When I tagged along with my mom to church, I hated the ritual, but I *loved* the faith. I eventually ditched out on the churchgoing because of my *fear*, which, too, came from the fact that I can believe in anything. Every time I hear about what different religions believe, I think, "That sounds interesting. That makes sense. I could buy into that." And that's scary. I had no filter for credence. I could throw myself with vigor into whatever the next charismatic person decided to preach. It's so arbitrary for me to open myself to that, and so I've gone the other way—I closed myself to it. I try to build a wall of skepticism against every idea I hear.

I wondered how my parents would feel if they could see me now and I couldn't help but wonder how my unit felt about me too. I hoped that they didn't hate me, and I hoped that they didn't pity me. I'd be happy to just be forgotten. Just a lonely roamer on a sorry mission.

The thought of that mission sent me into that all-to-familiar brief panic, and, in a frenzy, I made sure that Jude's letter remained dry in my pack. It did. I only read it the one time in Memphis, and so now, sitting in Kansas, I tried to recall its contents again only to begin thinking about the ghost of the woman who I'd be delivering it to. I'd never so much as seen a picture of her before, and I wouldn't have been able to recall her name if I hadn't seen it plastered on the outside of Jude's envelope. He would video chat with her from overseas any chance he got, but I was never around during those conversations. I hoped that she was easy to find, but realized that with them having no kids, and both being from somewhere out east, that she might have packed up shop months ago when Jude died. I moved that notion quickly from my mind—not wanting to consider the consequences of having to travel God-knows-how-many-miles in order to find her again—and mused on the moment of handing her that letter. She would have already gotten the news long ago, so I didn't have to be the primary heart breaker. But now I focused on different problems. Had she been expecting something like this letter from Jude in those months since his death only to feel disappointed and forgotten by her now-deceased husband? Had she used those months to mourn her lost husband and were the scars now beginning to heal? And would I tear open those scars anew with my delivery? Had Jude ever said anything about me to her? Would I even tell her my real name now that I was a fugitive? As the anxiety from these questions began to grow within me, the storm finally let up. The rain ceased completely and the lightning and thunderclaps slowed to intermittent bursts, and in that damp silence I found some rest.

I awoke in the heart of the night to find a spotless sky as monumental as the departed thunderhead. Not even in the Iraq desert had I seen stars like the ones I saw that night—more than I ever knew were there. I don't know how many of the things are out there, but I think from my spot in Kansas I could see every last one of them. I was still exhausted, cold, and wet from earlier, and so I stripped down to my underwear and hung the wet clothing between the slats of the windmill. It was a nice enough summer evening, but in my damp and nearly naked condition, I didn't have a prayer of keeping warm by just sitting on the wet field. To pass the time and keep warm while my clothes dried, I took it upon myself to go for a little run in my adopted acre. Like a lot of things, I don't know shit about agriculture, and the function of the field, other than housing my windmill, was lost on me until I made it around to the opposite corner of the thing. There I discovered the crowded forms of a dozen or so cattle, and figured that the field was where they were intended to graze. Now, all I knew of cows was that they were slow, passive creatures, but as I crept in on them my heart began racing just from their sheer size. A few of them stirred and chewed on whatever it was they were chewing on, but I marked the majority of them to be asleep where they stood. This triggered vague memories within me of seeing wild teenagers in movies pushing over sleeping cows and getting quite a kick out of it. I crept up to one of the sleeping creatures and ran my hand across its rough and spindly hair. I gave it a nudge, and then an outright shove on its front shoulder blades and didn't get so much as a budge from the sleeping giant. I attempted, from the same spot, to rock it until enough momentum was created that I could push it over at one of its peaks of swaying, but I could not generate enough motion from it. Now, I was determined to tip this cow if there was any chance of doing so, which there didn't seem to be, but I was going to play my entire hand before I gave up on the venture—that's how I found myself backed up about ten yards, in nothing but my underwear, charging full steam at the gut of the animal. Above me was the most picturesque night sky I'd ever imagined.

I hit the cow and dropped like a sack of bricks. I was probably lucky not to break a bone, at least, but my self-esteem wasn't aided by the fact that the cow didn't seem to mind me in the least bit. It awoke from its sleep just enough to move a couple of feet from my fetal-positioned form and presented me with its repugnant backside with its tail carelessly flipping back and forth. I took a few minutes from my position on the rough grass to gather myself and make sure my body was intact before giving the cow one last pet and returning to my jog.

At the next corner of the field I could see what I believed to be the house of the landowners. About all I could make of the thing was that it was one story tall and that none of the lights were on—and that was good enough for me. When I made it back to the windmill my clothes were still plenty wet and so I took a couple more laps along the field's fence line before I noticed the sky beginning to lighten. I hustled back to my pack and pulled on my outdoorsman pants. I hung the long-sleeve shirt, socks, and shoes from the back of my pack and, after I unzipped the bottom half of my pant legs, I continued my journey west, barefoot and tired. When the sun rose, it did so at my back and to my indifference. I kept my eyes on the ground ahead of my exposed feet and admired the length of my shadow splayed out before me. Within it I walked, and I kept my path parallel to highway 70 that busied itself only twenty yards to the south of me.

My slow pace gave me plenty of time to consider the many billboards posted along the interstate, and boy were they something to consider. The first one that I passed had the ever-popular luminous face of Jesus Christ on it, and it was tagged with the text: *I miss hearing you say, "Merry Christmas"-Jesus.* I didn't have more than a few minutes to ponder why, exactly, Jesus missed this exaltation so much before I saw another one rise in the distance. This billboard was apparently from God, and it said, *"We need to talk"—God.* Now I don't know about God, but whenever someone in my life said the words "we need to talk," I knew it wasn't going to be a pleasant conversation, and so if the purpose of that billboard was to bring people to God, I thought it was doing a poor job. Right behind that one was a woman hugging the robed form of Jesus and its message was simple enough: *Jesus, I trust in you!* That message seems better fit for a private prayer, but maybe this is how the Midwest prays now. And then: *Jesus Saves and forgives, Pornography destroys and enslaves.* This particular billboard was accentuated by a beautiful man and woman who were both scantily dressed, and as I stopped for a minute or two to admire them, I decided that it sent a rather mixed and confusing message. And after that? It seemed like the farther west I walked, the stranger the billboards got:

> *Are you missing Jesus in your life? www.missingjesus.com.*
>
> *Would Jesus chain his dogs? Dogs deserve better.*
>
> *Jesus heals cancer.*
>
> *"As my apprentice, you're never fired"-God.*
>
> *Can I be tight with Jesus and still have tattoos?*
>
> *The Bible is God's Facebook.*

I enjoyed what I thought to be the particularly clever, *JesUSAves,* accented with red, white, and blue starred letters, and the one I'll never forget? The ultrasound picture of a fetus sporting a halo with the caption, *"My Mother Mary said YES to life"—Jesus . . . Happy Mother's day.* Wow. What the fuck? I hadn't been to church since my parents passed, and I wouldn't argue with someone who accused me of being a nominal Christian, but I'd sure use those billboards as a reason for my spiritual departure. It was a poor attempt at selling gods like they're cars. I saw no dignity within those displays. They cheapened something that should never be cheapened. They attempted to commodify spiritual wellness, and if salvation could be found on a billboard, then how much could it really be worth? That's the message I took from all those ads. Not everyone is fit to spread any message, and many messages take their power from the very people that minister them. And if someone is genuinely going to missingjesus.com then they are missing a whole lot more than Jesus—and I can attest to that without the help of any billboard.

When the sun reached its peak that day I ducked into a row of corn with the intention of taking a long nap among the shadows and the cover of the rough husks. But before I could pass out in the cool soil, the last forty-eight hours ran through my mind—a storm of which I never knew the likes, a night sky of which I never knew the likes, and a string of billboards of which the likes I never knew. The least surprising thing to happen to me in those two days was me damn near breaking my shoulder on the gut of a sleeping cow. Ultimately the billboards faded from mind as I recalled the majesty of the Kansas sky and my suspicion of where one really needed to look in search of sanctity—hid somewhere out there apart from our knowledge where the storms and the stars are summoned for the watchers and their search for some divinity.

Buried in the Soil

The field of dead sunflowers ran the eastern edge of the graveyard where Silvio and the old man sat. It was as if the plush graveyard had sucked the life from its neighbor the way that a vampire does with blood. Their compromised stalks and shriveled black heads all faced east into the face of the distant setting sun. The large heads of the decrepit vegetation hung limply and their formerly yellow pedals curled to a deep brown color and fell drily to the ground below. They looked like a brigade of lost souls marching their way to the calling Hades. But it wasn't dissolution that awaited them, only the baking sun that they once grew to be just a moment closer to. Here is the real measure—Icarus had what was coming to him, if anything. But that field of flowers?

Mrs. Crawford told me you were spending a lot of time here, the old man said.

Silvio shrugged. He said, She said the same thing about you.

The old man ran his aged hand over the ragged stone of the bench they sat on. Silvio's parents weren't buried anywhere near where they sat, and the old man knew it. He said, I have a lot of friends here. Why do you come?

Silvio gestured to the gravestones with his chin and he said, I like to keep them company.

Keep who company?

The people.

It looks to me like these people here have moved on.

Silvio said, Maybe some of them haven't.

A light breeze blew between them and Silvio glanced at the neighboring sunflowers and at the old man and then back at the engraved stones. They were carved full of numbers and names and titles. Beloved sisters.

Loyal brothers. Loving mothers and devoted fathers. Silvio and the old man. A late summer afternoon.

Silvio said, Why is it that you come again?

To pay my respects.

For weeks now, the old man pushed for Silvio to take a formal approach to his life within the church. And the more the old man pushed, the more Silvio became set in his decision not to. In a constant state of passive aggression, the old man brought him information on seminary life and costs, the university courses he had taken that could transfer into a theology degree, and the process for becoming a deacon, if he thought the priesthood didn't suit him.

Silvio said, You think I should be a priest?

Yes.

After what all those priests did?

The old man said, Those priests are bad apples, Silvio. You aren't.

I think I'll stick with what I'm doing.

But why?

Because I've never heard of a saint that rapes kids.

The old man cringed and dropped the subject for a few days, but then began pushing the idea of joining a seminary as forcefully as ever. Silvio obliged him with smiles and assurances that he would look into them, but he never did. Near the end of July, almost two years since his parents' deaths, he arrived at the church with the news that he had sold his parent's house, and old man commented that he hadn't even known it was for sale.

The old man asked if that's what his parents would have wanted, to which Silvio said: I think they would have wanted to live in it.

Silvio moved into a dingy studio apartment on the north side of town and used the cash influx from his parents' house to start a church program that he called the rucksack project. He asked Mrs. Crawford to identify congregation families in dire financial situations that the church could possibly aid. She referred seven family names but insisted that during the Christmas season the church had a gift exchange program that was specifically intended to help out families like this in need. Silvio insisted that it wasn't enough and pressed her with approaching the families with the intention of giving them additional help, anonymously and more consistently. Two of the referred families turned down any additional help, and the other five were given instructions to provide Mrs. Crawford with a list of any ends that they were finding particularly tough to meet that week or month. All they had to do was leave a car door unlocked when they came to church on Sunday, or leave an address with Mrs. Crawford if they were unable to attend the weekly service. During masses, Silvio would slip out the back of the church for a few minutes and place in the families' cars a backpack filled mostly with grocery foods, but occasionally supplemented with cough medicines, toilet paper, sandwich bags, and whatever other amenities were specifically requested. By the time a ragged and homeless ex-soldier had made his way into the neighboring state, Silvio had only contributed nine-hundred and thirteen dollars to the rucksack project, and the pedestal in the garden still held no statue. By the end of August the number of families and Silvio's contributions had doubled, and by the eve of Patriot Day, as Silvio sat alone in his apartment and read in his Butler's guide, he was integral to spreading the word and the eventual project's expansion to four different churches that assisted thirty-two families with the financial support of fourteen benefactors. By the following spring, plans were made to expand the project to within the school district with the purpose of further helping community members in need. With the money from selling his parents' house, Silvio arranged to automatically deposit money into the program every month, and made three sizeable contributions to the public library, the animal shelter, and the local fire department. He didn't tell anyone, but the inspiration for the project came from his decision to begin fasting, and he was faced with a pantry full of food that he wasn't eating. Within weeks he was noticeably thinner and branded by dark clouds that hung under both of his eyes. When anyone asked about his apparent physical decline, he said that he felt fine.

Three weeks after starting the rucksack project—one week after protesting the abortion clinic with Vera—he walked through town under the light grey cover of a late afternoon rain cloud, and found a spot sitting on the front steps of church when he could not find the old man around the other parts of the building. He sat there for the better part of an hour as the clouds went to work and the concrete around him began to darken and dampen with the addition of the falling moisture. Silvio moved his back to the church's front doors, where the overhang of the building's roof kept him dry. He was hugging his knees and staring out horizontally at the lightly falling drops when she appeared from her house across the street and moved toward him with a hooded sweatshirt pulled tightly around her frame. He admired the locks of dark hair that sagged out of the opening of her hood, offered her a greeting, and accepted her request to sit next to him. As she sat down she pulled off the hood, tucked her hair behind her ears and hugged her knees in the same fashion as Silvio while they soaked in the steady patter of the world around them. After a deep breath through her nose, she commented on how much she loved the smell of rain.

Me too, he said.

You aren't wearing a jacket.

I know.

Want me to get you one from the house?

I'm fine.

His eyes were on the dark and distant clouds above while she worked at picking pieces of lint from the sleeves of her sweatshirt. He gently rubbed at the goose bumps on his forearms when she spoke again. She said she was sorry about the week before.

Silvio flashed a confused look and asked what she was talking about.

About the ride home, she said. About what I said in the car—saying I hated God and all of that. I shouldn't have said that.

He shrugged. You don't have to apologize to me for that. You can hate whatever you want to.

I know that. I just felt bad about it. . .I don't know. It's like, I don't actually feel that way. I was just angry at the time.

Silvio nodded his head. He said, I could tell that you were upset when you said it, and I didn't see it to be my business to press any farther—I apologize if it came off as me ignoring you. And I still know it's not my business, but if you have something you need to talk about, I'm more than willing to listen.

Vera was slow and indirect in her telling, but she eventually got to the point where her husband of less than two years had gone to war and was killed in action. Upon hearing the news she had taken to some nights of heavy drinking and she had received, what she described as, a well-deserved drunk driving citation. After the offence, the school she taught at suggested she take an indefinite leave of absence while they figured out how to handle the situation. She stayed at home during the leave, and they officially terminated her contract at the conclusion of the school year in early June. She said she hadn't really been in touch with her own family for years, and that her husband's family resented her. She was a widow at twenty-three and didn't sign up for any of it. She never thought her husband had an itch to be in the military—to run off and put his life and future at risk for a war that she admitted to know nothing about—not knowing a thing other than that her husband had lost his life because of it, and that was enough of a reason to hate the war and everything having to do with it. If she had gotten involved with Jude knowing that he was military man, then that was different, she said—that would be a decision, and she could live with a decision. She cried. She said she hated Jude for leaving her the way he did, and she hated herself for being the cause of it. She said that if he were happy with their life then he never would have enlisted—never would have fled from her. He was supposed to be a baseball player, and if he couldn't do that then he was supposed to inherit his family's ranch. She cried more and Silvio put an arm around her shoulders. Instead, she said, she had dragged him halfway across the country because she saw in those two possible paths a life that she could not live—and she knew that he always loved her more than she loved him. She said she knew that he would go wherever she would and so she came here. In leaving behind all the things she had never loved, she dragged him away from all the things that he did. She stopped crying. She said she hated herself for being selfish. Hated herself for killing Jude. Hated Jude for being too cowardly to face his own life here. She hated her sisters for never teaching her anything of value. Hated her mom for being so fucking sad. Hated the idea of her nieces and nephews growing up ashamed of their family, like she was. She hated herself for that shame. Hated Iraq. Hated whoever the hell Osama Bin Laden was. Hated America and all its exceptionalism. Hated anyone who said Jude died for liberty or freedom. Hated that Jude thought that dying for a country was more important than living for her. Hated her selfishness all over. Hated the counseling they suggested. Hated therapists. Hated being a widow. Hated having no family. Hated the Army. Hated whoever the hell killed Jude. Hated happy people and their happiness. Hated life and loss. Hated the prospect of her future. Hated the burdens she would now bear for the rest of her life. She hated all of it, and if God was all of it like Silvio had said, then she hated God too. That's why she said what she said.

The intensity of the rain remained consistent as the two sat undisturbed under and on the edge of their only shelter. She used the back of her hand to wipe at the redness that surrounded and infested her moist eyes. Silvio's goose-bumped arm remained around her slim shoulders as she apologized again for saying all of those things, and that she knew he really cared for the church. He told her not to worry about him. She gave a quarter-hearted laugh and said maybe he could write about her for a submission—about what not to do, and how not to be. He said that if he wrote about her, it wouldn't be about that at all.

It was a long time before Silvio spoke. He said, Did you know that the smell of rain isn't really the rain at all?

She sniffled once and said, What?

That smell comes from the soil mostly. There's a bacteria in the ground that dries out and settles down into the soil and it creates these little spores that get thrown into the air when the rain starts to fall. You would never see them and even if you were to get down on all fours and stick your nose in the dirt, you still wouldn't pick up on the scent. But as soon as it starts to rain those little spores that you didn't even know existed start to permeate the air. And that's compounded by the moisture in the air, because our sense of smell is strengthened when there is a lot of moisture in the air. Have you ever noticed how pungent all your soaps smell in the shower, when the room is all steamed up? The rain releases those spores and simultaneously creates an atmosphere through which to best experience them. The spores and your sense of smell are there at every other time of the year, and you can be fully aware of their existence, but that doesn't change the fact that you are going to have to wait for the first rain of the season to actually experience it—to realize what's been lying dormant and hidden there the whole time. And even after all of that—after the bacteria settles in the soil, and the soil dries out, and the bacteria creates spores within the soil, and the spores are thrown into the air by the rain drops, and the moisture within the air allows us to better smell the spores—one can mistake it all as the simple smell of rain. And you know what? The smell of it isn't any better or worse with or without all of that knowledge. That's just the way it is—the rain and the spores are going to be the rain and the spores whether anyone knows it or not. Crediting it all to the rain isn't going to change that—it's not going to change anything.

The rain Silvio spoke of continued to fall around them in its calm and persistent demeanor and she stared ahead at the dry concrete just ahead of her feet where the rain failed to fall as if the area around them had been demarcated by the ritual of some desiccated witch with a fatal allergy to water.

Vera said, Why did you tell me all of that?

Someone told me the same thing once. I just thought you should know.

Is that true?

Is what true?

All of that . . . about the rain?

Silvio shrugged. He said, I don't know.

Silvio Submission Eight:

THE CREATOR

On A Clear Autumn Night

If the stars act as freckles on his face,
and the Milky Way some incomprehensible nevus,
then the moody eye of the moon
would play the part of his peering focus

in placing the mast on a model ship
within the waves of an empty glass bottle.

I haunted the corn fields and the traffic of I-70 west of Kansas City for twenty-two days, by my count. Some days I'd spend my energy walking in the sunlight, some days in the moonlight, and some days I'd just sit and watch the late summer storms glide over the plains around me as I took them all in with a piece of bread and peanut butter. I got caught out in three more thunderstorms, but none of them took on the power of that first one. For two of them I was able to find shelter—once under the roof of some storage shed, and the other inside the cab of what I figured to be some farm's work truck. I was caught by surprise by the third one—I settled for using my jacket as a tarp for my pack, and took to another near-naked jog in the cool rain.

I braved the shoulder of the highway a few times and managed some success with hitchhiking. A Kansas State student—this one a journalism major—took me as far as the turnoff to Manhattan and commented that she thought I would probably make an interesting story for the school's paper—or probably any paper, for that matter. She said that she thought that most journalistic mediums tended to focus on negative stories intended to shock audiences and buy consumers—and it would be better if they would forget about the business side of the business and simply focus on telling the truth. I said that that sounded like a good way to do it. She agreed, and laid out her plans for starting a newspaper that wouldn't be restricted by those, what she called, trivialities—a pure and unbiased point of view. I watched the yellow and green fields pass by outside the window.

After another day west of Manhattan, a trucker picked me up and passed the time by telling me about playing in the Texas 2A state championship, fifteen years earlier. He was apparently a very accomplished linebacker and his team should have never lost in that championship game.

The referees put a real screw job on them, he said. The other team had gotten all the breaks, and one of his teammates had been called for defensive pass interference on a key third and long play that would have shifted all of the momentum their way. By all accounts, it was a phantom foul—a poor judgment call made by some man who had it out for them. He said that he'd never forget the pain of losing in that game. He said that sometimes at night, as he journeyed thousands and thousands of miles within the cab of his truck, he could still feel the energy from it. Still smell the sweat and the blood. Still hear the crowd. Still remember every play. He recorded six tackles, two for a loss, deflected a pass, and almost sacked the quarterback one time. Fifteen years could never take that should-have-been-a-sack away from him—hell, no number of years was ever going to take that from him. When we reached the limits of a town called Salina he dropped me off and said to me, Take it easy bud. And if it's easy. . .take it twice.

The city of Salina seemed to be big enough that I wouldn't draw unwanted attention. I bought three more loaves of soon-to-be-smashed-in-my-pack sliced bread at the truck stop, a plastic jar of peanut butter, a bag of powdered donuts, and the biggest fountain soda they had. For no particular reason I felt like a king that morning, and decided I'd make my way out of town on foot. I passed through the downtown area, which seemed summoned straight from a Walt Disney film, and as I neared the city's end, I noticed a rather indistinct sign and building that identified itself as a funeral home and crematory. Just a building that looked like any other building—any other business.

It made me think of the funeral home near where I grew up, and how it had one of the nicest lots of property you could find. It sat right in the heart of town, and monopolized its city block with a spacious parking lot, twisting concrete walkways, and a distinct architectural style that would be readily recognizable by someone who knows anything about architecture. It had wooden shingles and supporting posts, and its walls were a cream stucco material with a lawn adorned by well-groomed grass, gardens, and aged, black metal lampposts. As a kid, I often found myself wanting to go explore the many floors and hallways of the home, until was reminded by a hearse-led procession, or the black garb of mourners, that this is where the dead go to die. It didn't strike me until I was older how odd it was for a place like that to be so impressive. It took me a while to realize that there was an economy of death, and a thriving one at that. I'd never seen the home pay for advertisement space in the local paper, or on the radio either.

And why should they? Death doesn't need to persuade or spin or advertise. Everybody dies and they're always going to—that's a hell of a market share. Death is costly, and I don't mean that in terms of life.

I hoped that Jude's body had passed through a funeral home worthy of him. But I guess that once you are dead, you probably don't care much for what kind of funeral home your corpse is processed by. I always figured you just left all that shit behind you anyway. I was raised to believe that ahead of me, after this life, I got myself either an eternity of the good stuff, or an eternity of the bad stuff. By that estimation, whoever happened to be around could do whatever they wanted with my corpse. I obviously wouldn't be using it anymore, and if it can be used for some meaningful demonstration by someone who still has a body that functions properly, then they can have at it. But those people better get to it quick, because, as a serviceman, I arranged to be cremated—for dust I am, and to dust I shall return. Plus—and I mean this with all due respect—isn't there enough of a room problem in the world without reserving all this ground surface for people who aren't alive anymore? Can't everyone just be cremated and taken home by their loved ones and have it be left at that? Handling of the dead has always amazed me. I mean. . .a lot of people die every single day of every single year, and they've been doing that around the world for a damn long time—how have we not run out of places to bury them? This concerns me. Kansas and all of these states out here better watch out too, because I've seen how much open space they have and if there is ever a crisis of body burial, I'll be the first person to rat them out—that's a promise. You need room to bury a body? Take it to Kansas.

Anyway, I moved west on 70 from Salina for another week before I decided to depart from the interstate for good—depart into the wild North, as I imagined it. The highways that I shadowed for the rest of the way were two lanes wide—one going each way. The fields of crops I walked among now were more diversified than corn, and more frequently harvested the further west I walked. And more frequent were the fields with cows in them—lots of cows. The openness of the land and the country made me feel exposed and vulnerable during the day, and I swear I could feel the eyes of every passing car on the highway. I got the impression that nobody around here saw a lot of hitchhikers. I took that as a bad sign and took to travelling solely by night, because I hadn't come this far to get called in to the authorities, and I wasn't ready to start answering questions that didn't have satisfactory answers to anybody but me. That was the longest stretch I had gone without so much as talking to another soul, and when I made it to a place that I think was called McCrook, I loaded up my pack with as much food as I was willing to carry. I got more bread, but not the sliced kind, because the un-cut loaves didn't crush as easily. I topped it all off with more peanut butter, and granola-like bars that tasted like chocolate dirt.

I'd try to sleep during the day, sometimes under large and round hay bales that just sat in the middle of open fields and seemed to be neglected by whoever had rolled them. The more days I travelled on, the less flat the land became. It was easy to find little hills and juts in the land that, once the sun started to rise, I could simply go over to the non-highway-side of and sleep in the open air. Only a few of the nights got uncomfortably cold, and enough trees populated the land now that whenever a rainstorm passed through, I didn't have any problem finding cover. I don't know what kind of trees they were—the only kind I knew was the pine tree (which they weren't), and everything else was just another tree to me.

On a couple of days I noticed certain stretches of land where the trees seemed to disappear entirely, except for several dozen of the same sort that clumped themselves at the peaks of the highest surrounding hills—their exodus apparently justified by the extinction of their kin in the surrounding flats. They looked of shipwreck survivors clambered on a sinking island. Oh how they seemed to struggle for elevation. The one on the highest spot would be the last to be taken by the waves—those thirty feet of sunlight between the peak of the hill and the bottom of it appeared to be all the difference between top brass and total oblivion.

One day, after a particularly energizing chocolate-dirt bar and sunrise, I decided to walk along the highway for a few more miles than usual before finding a place to sleep for the day. I didn't hear the truck coming up the road behind me until it was too late. It crossed my mind to try to hide, but for fear of looking suspicious if I did so, I opted to keep on walking with my head down. My heart sped up as I heard the engine of the truck gear down, but my eyes stayed the dirt at my feet when it crept alongside me and a low squeak alerted me to the passenger-side window being rolled down. I heard an old lady's voice call me Son and then ask where it was I was walking to. I looked up to acknowledge her. Now, in all the time I had spent out there on my lone sojourn, I had never come up with a decent alibi to my travel. I had thought of the need to have a believable story if the wrong people should come asking, but I never could come up with anything good. I don't know if I just wasn't a good liar, or if I wasn't much for storytelling, or what the difference was between the two, but I arrogantly decided that I'd find a way say the right thing if the time came. Well, this was the time and all I could think of to do was tell her the truth. I told her the name of the town I was headed to and she asked if I was sure that I had the right town, and if I was aware of how far away that town was from here. I told her I was aware of both of those things and said that I'd already made it pretty far as it was and, speaking relatively, it wasn't really that much further by my standards. I told her it was my mythic quest. She measured me up and said she'd like to give me a ride to help out if she could, and I went with the old adage of keeping your friends close and your enemies closer—the longer I was in the cab with her, the less time she had to go wherever she was going and start telling people about some stranger walking around out in the middle of nowhere. So I warned her that I hadn't gotten a lot of sleep the night before and that I might not make for very good company. I threw my pack in the bed of the truck and climbed into its aging cab as she waved off my disclaimer and said I could sleep the whole damn way if I wanted to.

I didn't sleep a wink. I first asked her about the pickup, which she told me was the 1967 pride and joy of her late husband and she figured the truck to be older than me by a long shot. I told her it sure was. She gave a lovely and effortless laugh and said that it wasn't a nostalgia thing or a they-don't-make-them-like-they-used-to-make-them thing, but that he had always taken care of it and it had just kept on trucking. No pun was intended on her part. She told me that she didn't mind taking some time to give me a ride because she was more or less retired. Her husband's family had been ranching for four generations on their land, and he had turned just about everything over to his son before passing. Now she got to spend her time helping out where she wanted to help out, and giving her wisdom when she thought it was needed. She told me about her four grandkids and how she got to spend a lot of her time now just being grandma. I said I was sorry to hear about her husband but she laughed and waved me off—she said that she had gotten the best fifty-three years of her life out of that man and she expected to see him again soon enough.

We rode on quietly for a few more minutes when, before making sure that I knew full well that I didn't have to answer her questions, she asked me where I had come from and why I was going where I was going. I was taken by her charm and apparent harmlessness, and so I gave her a simplified tale of how I had ended up in the passenger seat of her pickup. I was honest about everything except for my desertion—I just told her that my tour was up, and hoofing it cross-country was my next adventure. She nodded and said she was sorry to hear about my friend Jude. She had heard it was a lot uglier over there than anyone expected. She mentioned that the war probably wouldn't help our image with the rest of the world, and maybe not with our own self-image either. That sparked a memory of mine, and I told her a story I heard from Jude, who told me about how some Chinese officials had once mistaken American porn films for torture films, and used their content to smear America's image in China. She laughed and said that China was an interesting country—that she thought it could be a great country if it would learn to care for its people. I said maybe the fact that it doesn't care for its people is exactly what made them so great in other areas, and she said maybe it was. Then I asked her what she thought about America.

She glanced over at me from the driver's seat and shook her head as she offered her aging chuckle and said, America. She said her late husband used to compare America to a great, aging athlete. For a long time it was indisputably great, and now that the rest of the world was catching up, it wasn't sure of its place among what it considered to be lesser and inferior talents. She thought that my generation was owed only a small apology—the prosperity that attended America in the post-World-War-Two world, which saw the ravaging of so many industrialized countries not named *The United States of America,* made its citizens truly believe that there was something intangibly great about their country. She compared part of her generation, and all of mine, to spoiled children. It is a country that built itself on the placebo of its own greatness. We expected prosperity and safety and innovation and equality and progression simply because we were Americans and forgot that the one of the great things about democracy is that it ensures that a country will never be any better than the sum of its citizens. I said I had never thought about it that way, and she said it was a good way to think about it—kind of like how Gandhi said to be the change you want to see in the world, except a little different. She said that instead of being the change, all the losers just whined about what the winners were doing with the power that the people weren't willing to grant to them, as losers.

Then she went on to say that she didn't give a damn, pardon her French, if twelve-or-whatever countries had adolescents who scored higher than America in math. She said math scores didn't make a country great now, and they never would. It seemed that America was focused on its greatness in terms of military power, but now it appeared they felt the obligation to put American boots on the ground anytime there was violent unrest in the world. And if we decide to not intervene? How long can we, as a country, watch innocent human beings die around the world, knowing that we could make a difference? And forget the military, she said—what about the food and the medicine that we have here in excess and all of the lives it could save in more desperate hands? She sighed and said the only way to live a happy American life was to not give a shit, pardon her language, about things that happen on the continent of Africa. She was quiet for a second and seemed like she was done talking, *But then again,* she said, each country has to find its own greatness—its own identity—and that can't be easy to do when the rest of the world is coming into your space and trying to fix you up in their foreign image.

I thought about the things she was saying when she went quiet for a few minutes. I told her that I didn't mean any offense, but for a retired ranch wife and professional grandma, she sure wasn't what I expected. She gave that lovely, quiet laugh again and said that I was sweet. She said that she had always had a keen mind as a young lady, but she came from a time when it wasn't easy for women to cultivate their intellectual attributes. She had never been an outlier—the Susan B. Anthony type—and when she fell in love with her future husband, that was good enough for her. Her husband loved to read anything about American history, particularly its military history, and she just loved to read anything.

We were quiet again for a moment when she apologized for talking so much, and I told her that I was enjoying her talking more than I had enjoyed anyone talking for a long time. She called me sweet again. She said that she thought if she had been born in a different time, then maybe she would have been one of those Susan B. Anthony types. She was sure that she would have gone to college, at least. I was sure she would have too. She said: the world at large shapes people into what they are. The men who fought in the American Civil War weren't born within them any desire to kill their own countrymen. The dough boys of the First World War weren't genetically more naive than you or I, but they couldn't imagine trenches and artillery and tanks and mustard gas from the world they came from. She said that the generation before her had been labeled the greatest generation ever by some, but she didn't think such a claim could be made about them. Did they not care if inequality ran rampant among its citizens of different races and gender and sexuality and religion? Was one great economic and military triumph enough to validate a country that wouldn't even let blacks use the same bathrooms as whites? The same drinking fountains? Was throwing Japanese citizens into internment camps during World War Two justified by our victory over Japan in the Pacific? I don't know, she said, but when people of her generation came of age, they sure had a heyday over things like that. She could recall the general attitude of people out here when the upheavals of the sixties were going on—how some found it annoying that African American's were fighting a cultural revolution in a country that didn't need any kind of revolutions. Why change the status quo when it was so dang good? Why couldn't everyone shut up and enjoy the prosperity inherent to every American? They were shaped by the greatness they were raised in and she didn't know if they could make it in a world after it. She said I was in the world after it—a world that had caught up to America's head start—populated by countries that had to be even greater than normal because of the years that had set them behind. They started building cars and electronics and toys that were better than ours because they had to be. The only advantage those other countries had in the global market was to make the best product—that's how *they* were shaped.

She sighed and apologized again for ranting, and I begged her not to be sorry. Then she said, Anyway, the world shaped me into a proud grandma and damn good wife and mother. I certainly could have fought to be something else, and I like to think I could have been whatever I wanted to, but that would have just been some other mold the world had already prepared for me. That's all most of us get, you know? Something the world is willing to accept from a person with our credentials—whether they be based on race or nationality or intelligence or athleticism or wealth or you-name-it. But there's always the special ones, too. The ones that the world has no mold for. They're usually tremendously good or tremendously bad for it, and they always leave their mark—even if it takes until long after they are gone to realize it.

I asked if she had ever met one of the special ones, as she called them. She thought for a minute and shook her head. She gestured to the empty countryside around us with her hand and said that the da Vinci's and Jesus's and Joan's and the Caligula's of the world didn't often find themselves out here. She laughed again and I smiled as much at her laugh as I did at the thought of some larger than life figure making his or her way in the back fields of Nowhere, America. She said bigger stages awaited people like that, and, though I wasn't sure if I was right or not, I said that I thought people like Jesus and Joan *did* start off in places just like this one—that this is exactly where they found themselves. Her grin was so big it hardly left room for me in the cab of the truck.

We drove on for about an hour longer without saying another word. The sun sat low in the sky and I still couldn't find enough fatigue in me to go to sleep. I stared out at the green and yellow land that now rolled past my window and occasionally worked itself into rock plateaus of varying size and expanse. In the flatter parts of the land I could see the black bodies of cattle as they dotted the countryside and immobilized themselves in groups with no recognizable rhyme or reason. In one field I saw a lone cow lying in the tall grass not within fifty yards of the nearest group of his peers. I wondered what one had to do to draw the ire of cattle, or if this one had even done that. Maybe he just liked that part of the field and they didn't. Were there extroverted and introverted cows? I don't know. In other parts of the land I would see packs of small deer-like creatures and I asked her what they were, exactly. She said I really wasn't from around these parts, and that those were antelope, and that I better get used to them because there were as many of them around here as there were people.

I asked her how close we were to the town that she was dropping me off in, and she informed me that we had passed that place awhile back. She said she was so grateful to me for listening to her rants, and that she felt so bad for going on and on with them, that she decided to take me all the way to my destination. I assured her that that wasn't necessary, but she was determined to do as much for me as she could, in order to help me with my mythic quest. She said it was just about another forty miles from where we were and I requested that she drop me on the outskirts of the town, wherever that may be. That won't be a problem, she said.

A half-hour later she pulled the truck to the side of the highway at the lip of a valley that cradled within it a small and unremarkable town. She geared the truck into park and told me that this was the place I was looking for. I don't know how long I sat there gazing at it through the truck's front windshield before I noticed her studying the side of my face. She asked if I was okay and I said I was. She asked if I needed anything else and I said I didn't—that she had done more than enough. She put the truck back into gear and flipped a U so she was facing back down the road we came from and when the truck came to a stop on the other side of the road, I creaked open the passenger door and grabbed my pack from the truck bed. Before I could thank her one last time and close my door shut, she told me to wait. She said that she had one more thing to say, and it was in regards to the antelope I had asked about. She said that they don't look like much, but they are the fastest land creatures in all of North America, and if you factor in the amount of time they can maintain their speed, then they are about the fastest damn things in the whole world. She asked me if I knew why the little buggers were so fast and I told her that I didn't. She said that there used to be cheetahs in this part of the world, a very, very long time ago, and that those antelope were either going to have to get fast or get killed. I said, Yes ma'am they would, and she said that just because the cheetah hadn't been around here for thousands of years, that didn't mean that the antelope were going to be getting any slower. I said, No ma'am they aren't. She said that as long as they existed they would be chased by the ghosts of their evolution. I asked her what she meant but she just said that humans were wired the same way—they had the tendency to run as fast as they could away from things that don't exist. I nodded.

She wished me good luck and said if I ever was in any trouble that I knew where to find her. I wasn't so sure I did, but I thanked her one last time and we said our goodbyes. I tried to figure for a moment why she wanted to tell me about the antelope like she did, but that train of thought left the station as soon as I turned my attention back towards the town that now sat washed at my feet. I was once again distracted by my quest and set in my purpose. I had finally gotten to exactly where I wanted to go and I had no idea what I was going to do.

Not That Garden

He said, I came out here in '79 to visit my brother and I thought there was no way I could live out here. I went back to Iowa and worked for two more years before getting discouraged and I told my wife I wanted to move out here. She said, I'm ready. So we came out here and me and my brother opened up a mechanic shop. But back at that time the economy wasn't any good. People needed work done but they didn't have any money for it. They'd come to us and want to get it done on credit but we wouldn't do that. So we closed up and I was looking for work and a guy I knew through the church said he might have something for me. He was the custodian at the church but he was about to go on a missions trip with his two boys and he asked me to fill in for him. I told him that I would and when he got back from the trip he asked me how I liked the job and I told him that I did. He said that I could keep it for a bit longer and I've been here every day since. That was something like twenty years ago now.

The old man spoke from the garden's stone bench as Silvio hunted the soil's weeds with a hand trowel and he shrugged at the man's suggestion that maybe some gloves would save him a little pain.

Growing up in Iowa I used to work on a farm. It was owned by a friend of my father and he agreed to give me work whenever he could. I'd have to go out into his fields with this single blade push plow, and that was about the hardest work I've ever done. It'd take all you had to keep it moving along but then the blade of it would get clogged up with mud and debris and you'd have to back it out of there and pull at the strike of it and you'd have to clean up the blade, otherwise it wouldn't turn soil like its supposed to. Anyway, one day the boss comes in and he's got himself a five-bottom plow to put on the back of the John Deere 4320.

The old man grinned and let out a low whistle. He said, That sure was a beautiful tractor. And I never had to plow again. Anyway, my brother ended up opening another shop just a few skips south of here, and it ended up working this time. He's still running it. He wants to sell the thing and retire already but he can't find anybody to buy it off him.

The old man looked distantly at the small houses on the blocks around him. He jittered his leg quietly for a few minutes and then he said,

It looks good, Silvio. The garden.

I know.

Does it have anything to do with your saint mission?

Silvio said, The garden?

Yes.

I don't think so.

How don't you know?

It's not up to me.

The old man tucked his hands into the jacket he wore and said, You've lost a lot of weight.

Silvio didn't respond. He was preoccupied with a root that he was trying to fishhook out of the ground between his thumb and forefinger. He cringed painfully as his hand burrowed deep into the dark soil and he strained back with the pinched root. It wouldn't budge and he sat back on his the heels of his feet, catching his breath.

The old man said to him, You can't use the church as a drug, Silvio.

What's that supposed to mean?

I've been around a long time and I've seen about every type of church-goer there is. And I've seen a lot of them that used the church and their religion like they would a drug. Instead of coping with what's going on in their lives, they use the church to retreat from it.

The old man pointed at the church building and continued, When that happens then this place no longer becomes a sanctuary. It only acts to disconnect the person from reality. This place becomes the home of sickness, not healing. It becomes a place of addiction and delusion.

Silvio shook his head and said, I'm not doing that.

He leaned back toward the ground to have another try at the en-trenched root. He muttered under his breath about where the root even came from and he said to the old man, There's no drugs in my life.

Silvio tossed a different small rut onto the path and waved at it with his hand as if to suggest he'd take care of it later. He brushed his hands halfheartedly on the legs of his jeans and then picked delicately at the soil that accumulated on the cuff of his long sleeve shirt. He took a seat next to the old man and again fanned his hands against his thighs. His hands were rubbed raw by the weeds he had pulled and the flowers he had sheared, and he gripped at the edge of the cold concrete bench to soothe them. A chill wind from the south gusted by the two and Silvio commented that he should have brought a jacket. He took his hands from the bench and rubbed at the small goosebumps on his forearms. He gauged the condition of the garden around them and then squinted into the western sky as if to measure the sun in the same way. The old man said again that the garden looked good.

Silvio said, It won't matter soon enough when the cold comes.

The old man nodded. Sure they'll die, he said. But they'll come back.

He was dressed significantly heavier than Silvio was—his frail body hid by the large jacket that gave him the dwarfed appearance of a child. The skin and scalp of his head revealed pale by the red star.

April is the cruelest month, huh?

What?

Nothing.

Silvio flexed his hands in front of his face and twisted his wrists to further inspect them. He rose from the bench and squatted next to one of the geraniums. He pinched it by the stem and adjusted its angle as if to look into the heart of the thing. He said,

What if we died like that?

The old man said nothing and Silvio dismissed the geranium and asked him if he was ready to go inside. The old man nodded and Silvio helped him rise from the bench. He used the young man's arm to stabilize himself and establish his gait as they made their way around to the sidewalk and towards the entrance of the church. He continued to lean on Silvio as they walked. And when he spoke he said,

They say that time heals all wounds, Sil, but what is one to do when time itself becomes the wound? You want to know what dying is, son? I've gone on the same walk nearly every day of my life for the last twelve years. On that walk there's a hill—a pretty good-sized hill. I used to like that part of my walk. I'd get to the top with a little burn in my legs and heavier beat to my heart and it made me feel good. It made me feel alive. For years it felt like that and I loved it. But the years passed and day by day I noticed it getting harder and harder for me to make it to the top. Then one night I got to the top and had to stop walking in order to catch my breath. That went on for a lot of nights before I couldn't even make it to the top of the thing anymore. It was too damn hard. I used to love getting up on that hill and just looking at the land and town below me. And now? I just avoid that part of town altogether when I walk—avoid having to see that stupid hill that I can't make it to the top of. You just wither away son. Day by day.

Silvio Submission Nine:

It's July in a nameless city anywhere in America, and two friends are playing tennis in a city park lost somewhere in their mid-thirties. They are average players—good enough to keep the ball in play for a few strokes, and bad enough that they get as much exercise in chasing balls over the fence as they do in actually playing the game.

On this day there is a mother in the same park with her young daughter. The child had never seen tennis before she bears witness to the two friends playing. Her small hands clasp the chain fence as she intently watches them perform the impossible with every stroke. She can't take her eyes off the bright ball as it ricochets between the scrambling women via fluid arcs and impossible angles. She would have admired the geometry of the game if she knew what geometry was. She may have compared the women's fluent whisks to Ben Hur or Leopold Stokowski if they weren't just the bizarre ghosts of some else person's memories.

The girl left the park that day imprinted with a passion for tennis that was otherworldly. When she went to Sunday school the next day, that child was confused by the cherubs that flew around with bows, arrows, and harps. She wondered where their tennis rackets were. She watched those women play for about ten minutes—which for a child is roughly ten hours, and for a cherub is about an eternity. Later in life she could not even recall this day or this moment. Nineteen years later, after she became the number one tennis player in the world, she would tell interviewers about tennis, *I just always liked it.*

And those two women she was watching? They didn't even see the child looking on to their court that day. Later that afternoon they ordered takeout and watched a tennis match on TV, having no idea that for ten minutes that day in the park they had become curious angels.

Years later, as the two women fought off health concerns and deterio-
rating bodies, they would watch the world's best woman tennis player on
TV. They were her biggest fan, in part because of the hometown that they
all shared. After watching her they would then head out to the park that
the girl made famous and try to emulate her every shot. It was the child on
TV—the child with the cherubs and neither's grasp of where they begin and
where they end.

I crept into the south end of town with my last stretch of sleep at least sixteen hours behind me, and still I felt exhilarated and on edge. I hadn't formulated any plan, but I knew that I couldn't deliver Jude's letter looking like I did—nearly a whole summer of dirt and sadness latched to my extremities. I could smell the insanity emanating from my filthy hair. Friday morning.

When I reached the valley floor from my drop off point, I came upon a small gas station that seemed to mark the unofficial edge of town. The name of the station must have been a local franchise, because I had never heard of it before. Set in a gravel parking lot were two gas pumps whose dollar and gallon amounts were represented with white numbers set on plastic black counters that ticked away the digits like an old speedometer. Inside the station was a young man behind a small counter preoccupied by the screen of his phone. He paid me no notice, but I still decided to buy a coffee for appearance's sake. He rang me up with minimal attention and I asked him if he knew of any storage units nearby. He gave me a curious glance and seemed to really look at me and my ragged costume for the first time. After a moment he said he only knew of one set of storage units in town and told me how to get there—the directions were easy enough. On my way out of the door I asked him if the town had a truck stop, and he said it was just west of the storage units I had asked about, on the highway that headed north out of town. I toasted him with my coffee cup and thanked him kindly before heading back out into the day and toward the heart of the small town.

I only had to walk for roughly three more miles and to take two turns down streets that were organized simply enough—E street, D street, B street—before reaching the storage units the young attendant had directed me to. They consisted of four rectangle buildings that were about the length of a trailer house and not much wider. They ran perpendicular to the street. On the non-street side of the buildings was the base of a rather steep hill that ran itself toward the top ridge of the western side of the valley and was empty of any residence until about halfway up, where there appeared to be a business sign that I couldn't make out. I appreciated the seclusion I felt as I approached the storage units. They were roofed with an ugly maroon tin and sided with a steel grey color of the same material. Along the walls were thin doors that looked like little garage doors, colored in the same maroon as the roof, and on them were three digits of black numbers. There were maybe two dozen little garages for each building. The sign in the gravel next to the buildings clearly identified them as self-storage and there was no fence around the property. I took out my bag there and looked again at the envelope gifted to me by Jude. Inside the envelope and etched into the key that I kept attached to the *Jones Brothers Realtors* keychain was the number 117. There wasn't anywhere near one-hundred-seventeen storage rooms in between those four buildings, so I don't know how they figured what they figured, but I found Jude's unit at the backside of the westernmost building. As I fiddled with the key to the unit, I spotted the large truck-stop billboard and sign about a half mile further west of where I was.

The contents of the unit were all but glorious. Again I was guilty of opening the door with the hopes of some great discovery being made, but there was nothing readily special at first glance. The only objects that were apparent in the small, rectangle room were a futon that ran along the right wall and an old dresser that faced it from the opposite side. Both items were pretty well centered length-wise within the unit, and so there was room both behind them and in front of them. I recalled Jude's note that the unit only contained items from his bachelor days that the married version of himself no longer needed, and so I managed my disappointment at its shoddy contents. I placed my pack on the floor next to the futon and, for the first time in a long time, I sat down on a piece of furniture and inhaled deeply. I closed my eyes there for a long while, and listened to the early autumn breeze blow past the storage unit's entrance. I felt my body in a state of rest. Even in the containment of the small room, my quiet heartbeat made no echo. My blistered feet.

When I opened my eyes again I turned my attention toward the back corner of the unit where an American flag draped over a box-like structure. Underneath the flag I discovered a rifle case lying pinned against the wall by a large plastic storage container. I peeked around the corner of the unit entrance to ensure my privacy and took the rifle case with me back to the futon. Inside I found a 243 hunting rifle and a tattered cardboard box of cartridges that still held half a dozen rounds. I checked to ensure the firing chamber was empty and held the rifle to my shoulder to feel the balance and look through its scope out the door of the unit and into the dirt of the hill. Jude had never said anything about being a hunter, and so I imagined the rifle to be for recreational and stress releasing purposes. I put the gun back in its case and propped it against the back shoulder of the couch before opening the plastic bin.

On top of all the contents inside the bin lay a Louisville slugger, lying corner to corner so as to fit properly. Beneath the slugger were several baseball uniforms folded on top of a number of cheaply framed team photographs. I slid the bin across the concrete floor so that I could dig into its contents while sitting on the edge of the futon. I placed the uniforms to the side and began taking out all of the photos that chronicled Jude's teams from tee ball to his final years playing in college. Jude was easily discernable in every photo—by his height and maturity in the adolescent photos, and by his confident smile in the more recent ones. I spread them in chronological order on the dresser before me and watched Jude grow.

Below the photos, at the bottom of the bin, were two baseball mitts and an unremarkable one-piece stereo that hardly seemed worth saving and storing. I opened and closed each mitt several times in my left hand and took in the smell of their worn leather. I placed the stereo and the bat at the back right corner of the cell and leaned the gun case along with them. I stripped my jacket and buttoned one of Jude's college uniforms around my torso—its material hanging baggy off my skinny frame. I placed the other uniforms back into the bin along with the mitts, draped the flag back over it, and propped all of the pictures, all seventeen of them, on top of the dresser.

When I stepped back outside the orange autumn sun was beginning to make its descent. I donned my pack and locked the door behind me as I made my way toward the truck stop just down the road. Upon reaching the parking lot I leaned my pack against a dumpster and began purging its contents. I tossed the three pieces of underwear I had rotated through the last stretch of the trip and threw in my one other t-shirt and long sleeve t-shirt that I had also rotated. They were dirty, they smelled. My rotation of socks was the worst. I debated getting rid of the pack entirely but thought that with a little cleaning it could still be salvaged.

Inside the stop I bought all the hygienic essentials. In the restroom I inserted quarters for one of the four showers and attempted to wash off my desertion and everything since. I used two cycles of the shower just to get a clean-shaven face, and then shut off the water in order to take a pair of clippers to my hair. They cost twenty-three dollars and ninety-three cents without tax. I buzzed my head and entered my money for another cycle in the shower—this time I rinsed my head and scrubbed at my body until my skin was raw. I used the remaining time with the water to take a bar of soap to my backpack. Back in the truck stop's gift shop, I bought myself some off-brand socks and underwear, a box of envelopes, a pen, a pair of jeans, and a couple of t-shirts with representations of bald eagles and American flags and wolves barking at the moon, respectively. My total this time around was fifty-two dollars and twenty-eight cents.

I carried my new stuff back to the storage unit, doctored up one of the new envelopes to appear identical to the one given to me by Jude, and debated my next move. Though I had no idea what it entailed, I figured I was too exhausted to deliver Jude's letter without some sleep. I still had plenty of money and considered getting a hotel room for the night, but as I laid back on the futon to go through my options, the more appealing it became to just stay put. I knew I could get in trouble for trying to sleep in the storage unit, but I had yet to see another soul around the property. On top of that, I was lucky that the unit was well secluded from any street traffic and the doors operated on an inner lock mechanism—not a padlock—thus allowing the door to be fully closed, with me inside, and appear like any other. I walked back to the truck stop and bought a flashlight, travel pillow, and a throw blanket. Batteries were six dollars and ninety-nine cents. When I returned to the storage unit, I closed myself in and slept in the deep black of its tomb.

I showered again the next morning and then began my walk toward where Vera was addressed to live. All the streets were intersections of numbers and letters, and so it was easy to find my way. As I passed through downtown, one of the bank's electronic signs informed that it was Saturday, September 13th, and the crisp morning air was fifty-nine degrees. When I realized I was walking down the street of my final destination, the weight of what I was about to do finally hit me. As I came upon the address, a man was walking out the front door, and so I panicked and walked right by the little house that shared the same numbers as the one on the envelope. As

I continued down the sidewalk I could hear the voice of the man begin to engage in conversation with a woman's voice coming from inside. I immediately panicked again, worried that I was going to look suspicious, and veered toward the church that sat directly across the street. People could go to church on Saturdays, I thought. But I didn't want to risk somebody actually being inside the church, so I opted to take a stroll around its perimeter for the purpose of buying myself some time to calm down and regroup. Around the corner I came upon a garden that extended from the back of the building. I wasn't much for flowers, but it sure was a beautiful garden and it conveniently contained an exquisite stone walkway and bench. Set against the building was a pedestal of some kind, but there was nothing displayed on it. I stood up and peeked around the corner of the church toward the house and saw that the man was still standing at the house's front door. The distance made it hard to see either of them too well. She appeared to be relatively short and him relatively handsome. Finally he said his goodbyes and flashed a smile over his shoulder and moved unintentionally toward me as he made his way down her front walk. My heart rate accelerated when I realized he was walking in my direction, but instead of making his way around the church and toward the garden, he entered the church.

Upon the garden's stone bench I took a seat and gathered my wits. I looked at the letter in my hands and thought about the date that flashed at me from the sign of the bank—September 13th. Not only was it disturbingly close to the 9/11 anniversary, but it also meant it had been more than two months since I had gone off the grid. Sometimes two months is a long time. Sometimes it's not. It also meant that this Vera—Jude's wife—was two more months removed from the initial news of his death. Would she be grateful to me for bringing this letter to her? Would she understand why it was coming to her the way it was? Who could?

Who was that guy?

It had to be done, I decided. And it wasn't right to send it in the mail—that's no way to receive news like this. I walked around the north side of the building this time, through the church's parking lot, with the letter gripped tightly in my right hand. Maybe she had moved. Maybe she had moved on. Maybe this wouldn't be so bad. Jude's wife. My Jude's wife. I was walking. My t-shirt sported a bald eagle gracing through the waves of an ethereal American flag. Her husband had died for this shirt. Or did he die for the eagle? It was for the eagle. He died for the flag. Who made these jeans? They were awfully made—a bad cut of the fabric, maybe. Was that guy her boyfriend? Had she already met someone else? The streets are empty. This was a quiet neighborhood. What kind of church was this? I liked that garden. Jude's wife is in that house. Jude who was dead. Me who is deserted. I should have gone to church more often. Desertion is my sin and this is my penance. America? Thine is the kingdom and the power and glory are yours, now and forever.

I knocked on the front door.

Space Enough

Silvio slipped out of the entrance of the church and walked through the cold and overcast air that settled in the valley. Alongside the outer wall of the church he ran a finger in the rough, dried mortar between the bricks as he made his way to a small vestibule on the building's northeast corner. He quietly entered. Inside he rummaged through the corner where the week's packs were prepared and stored. He hauled the packs out two at a time to the cars of the families for whom they were meant. When he had placed the last one inside its respective car, he tucked his hands into his sweatshirt and set his eyes on the house across the street. He thought to see less of her in the weeks following the trip to the clinic, the subsequent ride home, and her breakdown outside the church, but she only became a more familiar presence. She began attending weekly services and invited Silvio over for dinner on a near nightly basis—she said it was easier to cook for two people than it was for one. Between the church, the fire department, the library, and the animal shelter, he often declined, but couldn't always find an adequate excuse for not attending. And so he endured her admittedly poor attempts within the culinary arts. She usually enjoyed sneaking out of the service and helping him load up the rucksacks, but she hadn't arrived today, and from what he knew of her, he thought this absence to be incoherent with her character. He looked on at the closed shades of the house for another moment before shaking his head and re-entering the church. He spent the rest of the hour looking down at the roof of his left shoe while the quiet and slow droll of the priest's sermon interpreted the world around him.

When the mass ended he took on the handshakes and small talk of the congregation with a genuinely relieved bevy of smiles and spurts of laughter. The old man lingered near the entrance of the church as well, but the two of them didn't talk. When the crowd had finally dispersed to its other Sunday rituals of grocery shopping, football watching, pumpkin patching, apple picking, lawn mowing, bathroom cleaning, and cookie baking, Silvio trotted across the street and knocked on Vera's front door. It took a ring of the doorbell and another minute before she answered. He noticed that her eyes were red and swollen and asked if she was okay, to which she replied that she was. He wasn't sure how to proceed and, despite his better judgment, he asked if he could come in for a minute. She hesitated and he promised that it would only be for a minute.

I have to get home and feed a dog, he said.

She said, You have a dog now?

It's not mine, I'm just babysitting someone else's dog for the weekend.

So you're dog sitting?

If that's what you want to call it.

She shook her head and gestured him into the house. When she closed the door behind him, he continued to rest his hands in the pouch of his sweatshirt as he took stock of the room. At the center of her living room lay an open cardboard box—a large one—and still within it, and splayed on the floor around it, were dozens and dozens of framed and unframed photos alike. It only took a moment to realize they all contained the visage of the same unfamiliar face, and another moment to deduce who that face belonged to. Silvio pretended not to look at them too closely as she folded her arms across the chest of her bathrobe that covered her body. She rustled the unkempt hair atop her head but didn't say a word to Silvio as he continued to feign cluelessness. The silence hung for another minute before he said,

What's going on?

What do you think?

I think that your house is covered by photos of your husband.

He's not my husband.

What do you mean?

He's dead.

Silvio breathed in sharply as if to offer a retort but continued to stand quietly. Vera tapped her foot and looked absently at the far wall of the living room. Silvio asked if he should leave and she told him No. He then asked her if something had happened and she nodded her head.

Some guy came by here yesterday. Right after you left.

What guy?

Lewis.

Who's Lewis?

Vera threw her hands up in a gesture of helplessness and she spoke quickly. She said, I don't know who he is. Some guy that was overseas with Jude. He didn't say much. He apologized a bunch of times for a bunch of things I couldn't quite make out, and then he just handed me this letter. From Jude.

From Jude?

Yes. He gave it to this Lewis to give to me, and he said that this was the first chance he had to get it to me.

And?

And then he just left.

Silvio nodded his head and moved over to sit on the arm of her couch. Vera didn't move. Her arms were still folded across her chest and the red of her eyes faded to a bright pink.

Silvio took a hand out to scratch at his cheek. He said, So why the pictures?

Vera shook her head. I don't know, she said. I've just been going through them. I don't know. When I found out he was dead I put away everything that had his face on it. Keeping his trophy case over there made me feel better about completely ridding the house of his memory, but I couldn't stand to look at him. I didn't handle any of it well. I said and thought a lot of things I'm not proud of.

Silvio said what he was supposed to say: That sometimes death did that to people. That it was part of the grieving process. That she handled it as well as she could have. That death is a necessary and beautiful part of life. He said to her all the lines from self-help manuals and television talk shows and feel-good fiction that romantically traced the triumph of one human's soul, wisdom, and worldly knowledge as they encounter the inevitable and eventual death of someone important to them—how convenient those all were for the one who was not dead.

She nodded along while she sniffled and rubbed at the bottom of her eyelids with her right hand. Her voice was louder than before when she spoke again.

I didn't even go to his funeral, Sil. He was cremated and his remains were sent to his parents and I wasn't even there for the ceremony they had. His own wife wasn't there to see off her husband—a no-show at his funeral. What the hell? I couldn't face any of his family—not when I knew they would think that I was responsible for his death. And I was so selfish that

I didn't even show up. I thought it was all about me and my shame and my grief. And at the time I still thought that maybe I was responsible.

That's crazy, Vera.

She gave a frantic laugh and said, Maybe it is. But I felt like I had no business saying goodbye to him among the people that I dragged him away from. They never liked me for that, and they shouldn't.

Vera. . .

She shook her head slowly and tears began to come in earnest. It's okay, Sil. Jude's letter made it okay. Jude always made it okay. I could live a thousand lifetimes and still not deserve the love he gave me. But he's gone, and I wish I was gone with him. I don't want to be here anymore.

Her voice cracked and she said, Even from the grave he finds a way to comfort me—to bring me peace. And I couldn't even go to his funeral.

She wiped at her eyes with the back of her hand while she moved to the center of the room and began piling photos back into the box. She muttered to herself about how dumb it all was and Silvio rose from his seat to walk gingerly to the door. His hand rested on the doorknob for a moment before he turned around, put his hands in his sweatshirt pouch, leaned with both shoulders pressed against the wood of the portal, and stared into the house's kitchen ahead of him.

Silvio spoke slowly and deliberately. He said, There's this book I've been reading. It's set in Japan. Old Japan a few hundred years ago, I don't really know. Anyway, there's samurais in the book and, when certain situations arise, the samurai commit suicide—ritual suicide. Sometimes they are ordered to do it, sometimes they do it to avoid being captured, but sometimes they do it because it's an honorable way to die. Better to be dead than dishonored. It was hard for me to wrap my mind around that, in part because I don't value honor to the extent that they do, but it wasn't just that. It was the idea that someone would choose death over any other outcome. You're supposed to do anything you can to hold onto life just a little bit longer—that's how I thought humans were wired. But obviously that's not the case. It made me think about a life above which I would choose death, and I thought that maybe some lives are too terrible to live. It could be because of anything—physical disease, or emotional pain, or spiritual starvation, or not having access to clean water, or living in abject fear of someone or something, or being lonely, or a life-long prison sentence, or having the few things you love in the world all taken away from you long before they should be. Or it simply could be not getting to enjoy and appreciate any of the joys of life other than the simple fact that you are technically alive. I thought, why would someone be afraid to go to hell if they were already living in it?

She stopped putting photos back in the box and shuffled a handful of them between her hands. Her knees were folded beneath her and she sat on the heels of her feet. She turned her head and considered the fleshy plank of him there and looked back at the ghost in her hands as if to reference one to the other. One by one she began tossing them back into the box.

Silvio said, I don't think your life is one of these lives. I think you can live for a lot.

What do you live for?

Silvio pinched his brow in agitation and then gave a brief nod of his head and looked at the far corner of the room, avoiding any eye contact. He said, I live for a lot of things.

Name one.

The church.

Vera snickered and Silvio's eyes dropped to the carpet.

He said, What you've gone through Vera, I couldn't imagine. I don't know if you are supposed to start all over with someone else, or even if you can. Or maybe you are better off going it alone from here and trusting the pieces to fall into place. I'm probably supposed to tell you that your comfort lies in Jesus and in the Bible and in the church, but I know that that doesn't work for everyone—I know that. Sometimes that path just leads to resentment—people with whole lives telling you that there's a reason yours has been shattered. There may be a reason for everything, Vera, but there may not. And maybe it's not saying a whole lot coming from me, but you're the bravest person I've ever known for enduring what you have. I'll be here for you whenever you need.

Silvio straightened himself from the door and exited into the damp atmosphere. It hadn't begun to rain, but the air was so thick with moisture it was as if he stood at the base of a waterfall. He put his hands into the pouch of his sweatshirt again and considered the church across the street. He stood for a long time and looked at the heavy front doors and then raised a palm to feel the coolness of the water that had gathered onto his exposed cheek. He pulled the hood of his sweatshirt over his head and returned his hand to its dry den. He continued looking at the church across the way and considered returning to her house to further explain what he had said. He looked over his shoulder at the closed blinds of the house and the closed front door, and then he looked back at the church. He walked briskly along the sidewalks toward his apartment, away from the mourning home featuring a young lady brought to her knees by the misery of a cardboard box. Cold rain then began to fall in earnest. It only took a minute for his cotton sweatshirt to be soaked through. Soon the rain turned to ice, and small bits of hail thudded against the side of his hood and bounced like popcorn off the concrete and asphalt. He quickened his pace and he thought about Vera. He traveled through the neighborhoods of people who could make a thousand different cases for having it worse than she did. The world in all just countless personal prisons with space enough on the outside to tack the evidence of our triumphs, and space enough on the inside to carry every tragedy.

Silvio Submission Ten:

FOREVER WEST

The space between us could cause resentment,
but let not you and I come to grow cold
to each other. Let us embrace
the silence here and consider that without you
there is no me, and without me, you'd probably be just fine.

But, in case you aren't (fine), please accept a challenge
through this quiet space.
Go, my friend, and find the nearest place at least
seven-thousand feet above the sea. Be sure to arrive
at this destination in mild weather and on the clearest
night of year. Go you there.

Go to this place and think about anything but the stars.

I dare you.

For the conclusion of a mythic quest, it was quite anticlimactic. I knocked on the door and she answered and I can't even remember what I said to her before I forced the envelope into her hand and quickstepped it down her front walkway before transitioning into a dead sprint. I found my normal heart rate back inside my storage shed with the door closed behind me and the darkness all enveloping. I was out of breath, but as I caught it there on the couch in the pitch black of the cell, I went over the events of the brief morning—one thing I thought about was the man who had exited from the house. Was he a friend of hers? A lover? Neither? How long had she known him? Before Jude died? Was I angry? Had he stayed the night there or had he arrived not long before I did? He *had* gone into the church afterward, so maybe he was an employee there. A grief counselor or something. I don't know.

I should have skipped town at that point. I had no reason to stay. I had made it more than halfway across the country with as little incident as one could hope for, and I had completed my quest. Vera had gotten her letter—closure, I hope—and I had been the one to bring it to her. I hadn't let Jude down from wherever he was now.

But I had nowhere to go, and nowhere that I *wanted* to go. Delivering Jude's letter had been my singular focus for what seemed like a lifetime, so what now? I thought about what would happen if I were to just to turn myself in to the nearest military base. What happened to people that undeserted? It didn't really matter—they couldn't do anything to me worse than what they already had. Watch the most important person in your life annihilated right in front of your eyes and tell me what you give a shit about. Some people are equipped to move on from stuff like that, and some people aren't.

At some point I decided that I was going to be hanging around for a while longer, and because I had been uncomfortably cold the night before in the storage cell, I went to the truck stop and purchased a battery powered space heater and some wool socks. It was early autumn but from what I knew about this part of the country weather could be quick and unpredictable, and already there were some grey clouds camped overhead.

As I was checking out, a rack of books next to the counter caught my eye, and I opted to buy several paperback Westerns to help pass the time if needed. I dropped my spoils off at the unit and went on a walk to further explore the town and clear my mind. Just a mile or so north of my new home, I discovered a park set in the company of a handful of baseball fields. I found a spot on some empty bleachers and looked out onto an empty dirt diamond as I tried to consider why I felt hesitant to leave.

Instead, I thought about the time as an adolescent when me and a couple of neighborhood kids had come to fields a lot like these ones and smoked pot inside one of the dugouts. I'm sure now that it wasn't pot at all, but oregano or some other kitchen spice camouflaged by one of the kid's older brother's, pawned off onto his arrogant youth for a couple of bucks, because why not? That was us—rolling kitchen herbs into strips of printer paper so we could feel like drug users in the empty dugouts of the local baseball fields. And to think that some people actually did that shit—gave up everything to get the next high. Slept in dugouts and in parks because they had nowhere else to be. And really, I was the one living out of my dead friend's self-storage unit, so I didn't have a lot of room to judge except for the fact that I had no urges to take up heavy drug use as a hobby. Maybe my gateway drug was depression or anger or a lack of purpose. Maybe they knew something that I didn't.

I cleared my mind, and tried to focus inwardly on some very important questions. Was I depressed? Was I angry? What was my purpose? I closed my eyes and tried to will the answers to these questions from within me, but nothing came. My mind was foggy and all I could think of was how stupid it was to be a teenage kid trying to smoke pot inside a dugout.

I walked back to the self-storage unit, grabbed one of the books I had just bought, and headed back to the baseball fields. I sat on the concrete bench inside one of the dugouts and read until it was too dark to read anymore. After a cozy night of sleep in the storage shed, I woke to the sound of hail hitting the tin exterior of the building. It sounded like a bag of hard candy being dumped out into a plastic bowl. I stepped out of my room and gave a quick walk around the property to ensure that I was alone. The hail was small, and I discovered that being hit by it was exhilarating, unpredictable, and just painful enough to excite. There was nobody else around and so I returned to my storage unit, slid the door open, and soaked in the sight and sound of the storm. The tin material of the building made the storm sound much more violent than it was, but I found it to be soothing all the same. I thought for a long time about the day before.

The church. That's where I needed to go. Needed to? I don't know. Wanted to? I wasn't even sure of that. I was sure that if I got on with things now that I'd forever think about the young man who beat me to Vera's. I wasn't sure of anything other than I wanted to know who that was. That's all I wanted to know.

Encounters

The red brick of the church adopted a darker hue as storm clouds crept over the building's position, and inside the old man's eyes were opened by the sound of someone entering the nave through the main doors. Even for aging widows, early afternoon was a rare time for anyone to come into the church, and even rarer for someone he had never seen before. The man who had just entered took unsure stock of the room. He seemed to hesitate at the presence of the old man, but upon getting no reaction from him, continued to move into the church. Along the walls of the room, on both sides of the pews, hung a series of framed, stone representations that detailed the events that led to Jesus Christ's crucifixion, and his subsequent resurrection. To each of these the stranger lingered. He would pause for a few moments, muse on the contents of each sculpture, and move on to the next. He made his way around the room in this manner and not a word was exchanged between the two. Finally, after absorbing the final image for several minutes, the stranger spoke to the old man from across silent space.

Do you work here?

A little bit.

Do you mind if I ask you a question?

Of course not.

The stranger moved through the benches toward the old man and took a seat one row ahead of him. He faced the old man. His elbow hung over the back of the pew as he addressed him again.

Well, I don't know exactly what my question is. Maybe I don't have one. I mean, I never paid much attention in church as a kid, but I know about Jesus. I guess everybody knows about Jesus. It's just that I was looking at these sculptures and I realized how much I don't know.

The old man gave a small smile. He said, That can be a good thing. Some people, unfortunately, never realize that. However, you were right about the absence of a question.

He gestured to one of the representations across the room and said, I'm wondering if you can tell me more about the one of those called The Betrayal.

The old man said, You want to know more about Judas?

The young stranger hesitated then said, More about the circumstance than the man. More about the actual betrayal.

The old man's eyebrows raised in thought and he offered a small grunt to signal that he was mulling the question over. That is quite a long story to get into, and the Bible can tell it to you better than I ever could. I could show you the pages to read if you like—let you decide about it for yourself. I'm afraid I can't be much more help than that. Are you sure you don't have something more specific in mind?

The stranger's gaze rose from the floor between the pews and met those old eyes. He asked, Do people hate Judas?

The old man laughed and shook his head. He said, Judas is a highly disputed figure in the minds and voices of many people—his motivations, his role in fulfilling prophecies. His guilt. I could give you the church's official stance on the matter, but I don't think that you are interested in that, are you?

Not really.

Son, what's bothering you?

The young man shrugged and began to pick at his fingernails. He said, I used to have a very good friend, but he's dead now. We were in the Army together. His death wasn't my fault, and I guess it was out of my control. But, I don't know. I don't think it's like Judas, except that I feel guilty now. I feel like I've betrayed him. Or betrayed his memory, or something.

His eyes again rose from his fingernails and he said, I just saw that picture over there and it made me think of him. It made me think about Judas and wonder if I am like him. Before my friend died I thought the world was a pretty simple place. I don't know. I'm sorry I wasted your time. I don't know what I'm looking for.

The old man reached out and rested a hand on the stranger's forearm and gave it a friendly squeeze. Son, he said, I'm sure you are being too hard on yourself with all this talk about Judas. But if that doesn't satisfy you, then don't forget that Jesus *loved* Judas. He loved him before the betrayal, he loved him in the moment that it happened, and as each was strung up to their respective lumber, he loved him then too. Think of him as that friend who could never quite get it right. Someone that maybe caused you a lot of trouble, but a friend nonetheless. You are Judas, son. So am I. Everybody is except for those that can live up to the standards of Jesus himself.

The old man stopped for a moment and drew his hand back to himself. He then placed his hands, palms down, on the pew underneath each of his thighs. The stranger's head leaned over the pew and toward the old man's thin form. For a minute neither of them said anything, and an uncertain look came over the stranger's face.

The old man appeared to have fallen asleep, and the stranger uncomfortably looked around the empty church. But then the old man said, Bear with me for a minute—you just said that you thought the world to be a pretty simple place, but I think that maybe that's what's gotten you into trouble. What did you mean by that?

I just meant that, in the big picture of things, life wasn't supposed to be so hard. For a while you're a kid, and you play, and you get some scars from doing stupid things. Then you grow up a little, and there are girls, and you still do stupid things. Then you get a job, and you buy a house, and you start having kids that hopefully have it just a little bit better than you did. There was tragedy and war around the world, but it was never our tragedy. And people died in war, but it was never us who died. It was never us.

The old man nodded his head. The thick storm clouds outside played with the sunlight and shadows danced off of the colored window panes around the two in the pews. The old man admired the shade of green sunlight that passed over his pale forearm and then said,

Son, the world and you don't stand separate, with you trying to figure out some puzzle that it has to offer. There are no right answers. You and it are one. It's not just a rock with a cold, stony shroud. It's not some dream of Darwin's. And it's not some quiet and unreflect circle of life. It's made of the human experience. It's humanity that shapes it, and humanity that comments on its qualities. We're talking about the same humans that were made in God's image, sure. But we're also talking about humans that are infected with the devil. Every one of us is infected—I can see it in your eyes, son. And for that reason, it's a mess. If we're a mess, then the world is a mess. That's just how it is. And within that mess you are going to make mistakes. You're going to get lost. You're going to think you've got the puzzle solved a thousand different times before you realize that you don't even know what the ultimate image looks like. Just remember that Jesus stands behind you because he made the decision a long time ago that you are someone he is willing to die for, and when decisions like that are made they aren't gone back on. The old man wagged a wrinkled pointer finger at him and said, Pacts bound by death are not easily broken.

The old man stopped talking as the church's main entrance opened and closed again. Lewis recognized the entrant immediately as he strolled into the nave and glided across the dark carpet with his silhouette raked smoothly upon the cream-colored walls of the building's interior. The newcomer offered the two a slight hand wave of acknowledgement while he continued wordlessly into one of the back rooms. Lewis never took his eyes off of him.

Does he work here?

A little bit.

There's a lot of that going on here.

What?

People who do a little bit of working.

The old man laughed and said that Lewis must really not be from around here.

Why's that?

Son, if you don't know who Silvio is then you aren't from around here.

He's famous or something?

Or something.

Lewis offered a quiet grunt but probed no further. The old man asked if he would like to meet Silvio. Lewis gave a shrug of the shoulders and said, Sure. The old man rose slowly from his seat and walked delicately across the room and through the door where Silvio had vanished. Several minutes later he appeared. The similarities between the stranger and Jude were uncanny. They were eerie. The build and the eyes and the way that he smiled and the way that he walked—about him an air of Judeness. He entered the same row of pews that Lewis sat in and offered a handshake.

How are you doing?

Good, thanks. I'm Lewis.

Silvio.

He took a seat next to Lewis and folded a leg up onto the pew and folded his elbow over the back support, like Lewis, so as to better encounter him. They sat facing each other in the same row, incomprehensible and unrecognizable reflection of the other.

Silvio said, I like your shirt.

Lewis looked down to remind himself of the truck stop t-shirt he was wearing. It featured the prominent and impressive maw of a Bengal tiger, opened fiercely to any who dared look upon it.

It's one of my favorites, Lewis said.

Silvio nodded his approval and asked Lewis if he had ever heard of the Bali tiger.

Lewis gestured toward the tiger on his shirt and asked, Is this a Bali tiger?

Silvio laughed and waved at the shirt in a motion of dismissal. He said, No. That is not a Bali tiger. It's actually kind of messed up what happened to them.

He then explained how the Bali tiger had lived exclusively on a small Indonesian island and how it was hunted to extinction around sixty years ago. There were some grainy black and white photos of the small feline, but very few. And that was all that was left of it. A few bad photos.

Lewis let out a low whistle and said, That's too bad.

Silvio agreed and said, But extinction is nothing new. It happens. What's interesting with the Bali tiger is *why* it went extinct. It was hunted, which also isn't anything new, but it wasn't hunted out of greed or out of sport, you know. It was hunted due to superstition. The people that lived on the island with this tiger had a cultural custom, and the tiger was believed to represent evil and destruction. And, because of that, they went out and exterminated it.

Lewis chewed his bottom lip and said, I've never heard of anything like that before. It's a shame that they couldn't decide on a different, less graceful animal to put their burdens on.

You're right, Silvio said. But I think that the real shame is that they couldn't focus on eliminating *actual* evil and destruction, and not just some symbolic representation of it.

Lewis nodded and said, It's hard to argue with that.

Silvio offered a passive smile and waved another dismissive hand as if to apologize for his random conversation topic. He said, Anyway. Our mutual friend tells me that you were a military man.

That's right.

But not anymore?

Not anymore.

That's how your friend died? The one you told him about?

Yes.

Lewis shifted slightly in his seat, straight backed and eyes all over the room. Silvio studied him intently.

He said that you seemed to be having a bit of a crisis.

Lewis gave another barely perceptible shrug. He said, I guess you could say that.

Silvio nodded and gestured his hands to the inside of the church. He said, This is a good place to be in the time of a crisis.

Honestly? I wouldn't really know.

You're not much of a churchgoer I take it.

I'm not much of anything these days.

The weather outside the church seemed to still during their conversation. A cloud settled in the path of the sun and filtered the inside of the church into a lusterless noir.

Silvio said, In moments like those I find its best to just pray. Church or not, prayer can always have a soothing effect on one's undercurrent.

I wouldn't even know what to pray for.

Silvio nodded in understanding. He said, It's not always easy to know that.

What do you pray for?

Me? It just depends.

Okay. Well when is the last time you prayed?

This morning.

Okay, so, this morning. What did you pray for?

Silvio thought for a second and then he said, This morning I prayed for patience in all things. I asked that I be calm within the fury. I asked for the wisdom to guide those in need of direction, and for the will to resist temptation. And I prayed to be filled with the Holy Spirit. I prayed for God to cast out my demons, and for the strength to vanquish the dragon at my feet.

Lewis ran a hand over his buzzed hair and took a deep breath. He said, That's a lot better than the stuff I remember praying for.

We pray for what we need. It's different for everyone.

Lewis clasped his hands in front of him, as if in prayer, then motioned them back and forth like they held dice. He asked, You prayed for the wisdom to guide people this morning?

Indeed.

Okay. Here's your chance.

Silvio smiled at the stranger and then leaned back in the pew at an unnatural angle. He said, Fair enough. But you'll have to be a little more specific.

Lewis smacked his lips and rubbed together his clasped hands in willful pondering. He said, Let's see then. It's like, my friend was a good soldier. A good person too. He wore this cross around his neck, so I assume he was a religious guy as well. We never had that conversation, to be honest. But he was a nice, strong guy. A leader. And on the day he died? He didn't do anything wrong. He didn't break any protocol or get sloppy with his duty—he just got unlucky. I don't get that, you know? A guy does everything right, says all the right things, plays his cards perfectly, works his ass off, and then he's just dead. It's not supposed to be like that. Things like that shouldn't happen to good, innocent people. Twenty three years of living a good life shouldn't be undone in a meaningless instant. It's hard to make sense of a world where that can happen.

He gestured to the inside of the church and said, I can't make sense of all of this—of how God could allow things like that to happen. It's all so meaningless, so pointless. I don't know. It's not fair.

While Lewis was talking, Silvio had moved so he now leaned forward with his elbows resting on his knees and his hands interlocked. His eyes were focused on the floor between his toes. The sirens of an emergency vehicle could be heard from across town. He said, I agree with you that things aren't always fair, but that's no blemish on mine or any other God. It's Lewis, right? The heart doesn't beat different inside the body of a good person than it does in a bad person. It doesn't beat differently inside the body of a Christian. You have that body, and whether it's the shell for something greater or a vessel all its own, you can't use its misfortunes as proof of anything. You can't use it as an excuse for anything either. You can't use it to hide from Him, or to deny Him. And he doesn't simply sit on high and lend out badges of invincibility—people are going to die. Tragedy is all part of the plan, even when it seems like chaos. He doesn't gift us a world without pain and evil, because such a world would be an insult to *our* spirit—our soul—which would be given no opportunity to grow. We'd have no opportunity to be brave. We couldn't forge the steel of our perseverance in the absence of things that daunt us and disturb us. My friend, I ask you not to wither because of the disaster that kills good and innocent people—good and innocent children. God will take care of them. He's God. You can be sure he can take care of people long after their return to dust, and you can be sure that when he makes a world where terrible things happen, then that is the only kind of world worth living in. Let the dead bury their dead. What do you know of suffering that he cannot? Who are you to determine what's fair against his credentials?

It was Lewis's turn to eye his counterpart, who continued to hold his deflated pose. Lewis said, I don't know. I'm not anybody.

Silvio looked over at him and said he was sorry. I didn't mean it to sound like that, he said.

I thought it sounded pretty good.

A wry smile from Silvio. Thanks.

And. . .you don't work here?

No.

Do you mind if I ask what you do?

Not at all.

Lewis popped the joints in his fingers again and sat silently. The silence hung for a moment before he said, So what do you do?

I guess you could say I'm a professional volunteer.

A professional volunteer?

Yeah.

You just really like volunteering?

You could say that.

What would *you* say?

I'd say that I'm trying to become a saint.

Come again?

A saint.

I don't follow.

Do you know what a saint is?

Like Mother Teresa?

Yeah, like that.

Yeah, I know who Mother Teresa is.

Okay. Like that.

Lewis nearly burst into laughter, thinking himself the victim of a ridiculous joke, but, before letting loose he processed that he wasn't being toyed with by his new acquaintance.

Lewis said, You're serious?

As a heart attack.

Lewis tilted his head and said, I've never heard of that before.

Silvio shrugged. Not a lot of people have. Are you living here now?

I'm just visiting.

For how long?

Just a few days, I think.

Silvio nodded. The sirens had faded from sound. The old man appeared again out of the room where he had first retrieved Silvio, and he crossed behind the lifted floor of the altar and into an identical looking door on the opposite side. Seconds later he appeared again with a small vacuum held to his chest as one does with a small child. He crossed the altar again and vanished again in the first room without so much as a word. When he closed the door behind him, no sound of a vacuum issued forth. The silence between the two of them was filled from outside the church by the soothing pitter of raindrops on the building's roof and windows. The falling water assembled by way of its peculiar magnetism and slid down the stained glass windows in patterns that joined and streamed in a preordained manner that was unrecognizable by any who looked on it. When Silvio spoke again, Lewis was unsure whether it was a question or a statement.

Vera's husband was the friend that you lost.

Lewis caught his breath sharply and said, Jude.

That's right. Jude. Silvio nodded his head, and then he shook his head, and then he said, Anyway, Vera has become a good friend of mine and he sounded like a good person. I just wanted to offer my condolences to you. I'm sorry that you lost your friend.

I appreciate that.

Silvio rose to his feet and offered another handshake to Lewis. He said, Listen, if you find yourself getting bored around this town, don't hesitate to come back around. You're good company, Lewis.

I appreciate that too.

Oh, and the church hosts bingo every Monday so if you're looking for something to do tomorrow night, feel free to stop by. We have it over at the city center in the old gymnasium.

I might take you up on that.

Silvio offered a departing nod and headed into the room the old man had most recently entered. Still no sound of a vacuum. Lewis turned his body in the pew to face the front of the church alone. He looked up at the church's fans and at the altar and the presider's chair and the pictures and the pews and the cry room. He folded his hands into his lap and listened to the tapping of rainfall against the nearest window. He saw no lightning and he could hear no thunder, just the steady drowning repetition of the sky's mild assault.

He sat there alone for a spell. By the time the rain stopped and he made it back to the storage unit, the sun had descended over the crest of the earth, marking the horizon with shades of pink and orange before submerging into the depths at the far side of the earth. Lewis closed himself inside the unit and read a Western by the light of his flashlight. When the poor lighting had strained his eyes beyond the point of comfort, he slid open the door of the unit and stepped outside to the night. The storm clouds washed the sky clean, leaving in its wake the countenance of the universe. He walked to the corner of the street to stretch his legs and took in several deep breaths. Directly above him was one of the cities many street lights, and as he looked up to consider the endless universe, the lamp of the light dominated his earthly optics—blind agent without the tools or the appreciation to be overwhelmed by any of it. The entire cosmos finagled by a single street light.

He got back to the unit with his head down and laid it on the arm of the old futon. His eyes locked on the ceiling that he couldn't see but he knew was there. He tried to look beyond it. He tried to look out there—beyond the street lights and the planes and the satellites, where the light of burning stars travels for untold years before giving a living soul any fair glimpse. He wondered how long he could peer at the heavens before realizing that every last one of the frozen wonders was dead—smothered out with only their last hurl of light as proof of their passing. He admired how they blazed in defiance of the drowning cold that assailed them and lamented their inevitable expiration that took along with it all the dreams and wishes so vainly placed on their lamp-like orbs—riding on the final rays of light that originated from the middle of some mysterious black nowhere.

Silvio Submission Eleven:

PRAYING

It starts on a fall evening
with a prayer for the family down the street
who recently lost a son to the consumption of cancer.

It asks the lord to shepherd over the family—theirs and mine,
names spilling forth as if recited from the first chapter of Matthew.

Next comes the ragged line of those
in the latest natural disaster
searching for loved ones,

followed closely by people locked
into the chest of war,
and those who carry the key.

Slowly strangers' faces begin to circle,
summoned from local vagabonds and the evening news cast.

Feeling the guilt of having left someone
in crisis out of this growing pond of a prayer—
like a true pageant princess I ask for world peace
and an end to all drought and disease and hunger, please.
Please don't let this wish for that family
and their son be lost in the cresting waves

I've tried to hold back with quick incantations,
the perceptible moving of my lips lost
in the sign of the cross
I now make to bring an official end to my plea.

The thing that I never got out of these Westerns is the logistics of the entire operation. I know that part of the deal here is that I suspend certain modes of belief as I enter into a fictional world, but I can't suspend the belief that these cowboys are human. What and how often do they eat? How often do they get the chance to bathe? Do they carry a bar of soap around with them? Because if they don't, then continually bathing in river water doesn't seem that great. What's their purpose, in general? Where do they get their haircuts? How much do they pay for a haircut? How many different styles of haircut are available to a cowboy?

And here's the big one . . . wiping their asses. I don't know if I got into this during my own journey or not, but I want to make clear that I always had a roll of toilet paper, or a pocket pack of tissues, or something that I could wipe with after laying down a john. If you aren't in a position to wipe your ass clean after laying some brick then you need to rethink your life, and that's how I feel about these cowboys. And another underrated part of the whole cowboy enterprise is that these guys are degenerates of the worst kind. They have no homes, no families. They drink at any chance they get and we've already established that they must smell awful while their doing that drinking. Go out to your local watering hole and sit next to someone who smells like cow shit and dried sweat and stale whiskey, and I challenge you to have a positive thought about that person's life decisions—you won't. And the ones who aren't authored by some guy with a romantic erection for cowboys and get to score with the local babe, they have to settle for whores. They had to settle for the company of whores at a time when venereal disease was at the peak of its powers. Oh, and they gamble a lot too. And if they don't smell like cow crap or their own crap, then they smell like bonfire. That smell is a real pain to get out too. It's convenient to leave all of this stuff out of the tale and paint these guys as the portraits of rugged heroism, but I'm not falling for it.

And here's the other big one. . .people always think they would thrive as one of these characters. They romance the idea of being a super individual and living off the land and sleeping under the stars every night. They're so blinded by the dream of it that they forget about the reality. They forget about the grime and the smell and the insects and the heat and the crippling loneliness and the medicine. . .don't ever forget the medicine. If you manage to get yourself shot in 19thcentury cowboy-world and you're lucky enough to have access to one of the handful of actually educated people, then you're going to drink some whiskey as a painkiller and have some guy who hasn't operated on anything other than cadavers, if anything, his entire life, and he's gonna go fishing inside your body to pull that bullet out. Oh, and hopefully he disinfected the instruments and actually washed his hands and the "operating room," because who knows what people really learned in medical school in the nineteenth century. I want the readers of these books to appreciate how terrifyingly painful nineteenth century surgery would be. Good god, archaic medicine scares the life out of me— leeches, mercury, bloodletting, trepanation, and so on. They used to try to cure male impotence by shocking the penis with electricity. Nope. But in all fairness to cowboys, I served with a handful of guys who would have embraced and thrived in that degenerate lifestyle. They wouldn't mind being perpetually filthy and outdoors, and spending their days and nights of travel looking forward to the next drink and whore. Drinking whiskey as a precursor to caveman surgery wouldn't deter them for a second—they'd probably drink whiskey before surgery anyway. I sure respect them and they're the kind of guys you want to be in the trenches with. This will sound wrong, but I like to think of them the way I think of dogs—I'm a little revolted when I see a dog rolling around on a dead fish, but I'm comforted by its presence because of its heightened awareness and its instincts of loyalty and protection. There's something about that—being comforted by the knowledge that the people that surround you aren't the least bit like you. I was a subpar soldier and I like to think that I'd die for my brothers in arms if I had to, but I still wouldn't feel comfortable to know that I as in a company of Lewis's. That's just too much Lewis. There'd be too much faux bravery, bad luck, and indecision for that company to make it one day through any war. But the cowboy soldiers? Those are always the last ones standing, naturally. They're the type of guys that people find ten years after the war is over, hiding in caves and subsisting off of mushrooms and moss and preparing for the next wave of enemies.

Anyway, that's the kind of stuff that I ran through my mind instead of having to think about my encounter with Silvio. A saint? What on earth is that about? There were five different times that night where I tried to convince myself that he was just messing with me and that he just had a particular and hard-to-grasp sense of humor, but I never came around to it. The look on his face and the tone in his voice replayed in my head and I knew he was serious. And then what was Vera to him? A church project? A support group? A friend? A saint? I said it to him and I'll say it again—I've never heard of anything like that before. Those minor questions turned with me in the darkness of the storage unit all through the night.

The next morning I hit the truck stop for a shower and then I headed to the church to try for a chance encounter with Silvio, which is exactly what I got. He was in the vacuum room loading up a bunch of backpacks with food, but he asked me if I'd like to grab some breakfast and I obliged. We walked several blocks to a diner located in the middle of a postcard-like main street, and over a couple of plates of scrambled eggs and bacon, we exchanged our histories. We talked through our plates, through our toast, and through three cups of coffee. There was nothing extraordinary about him, by my estimation. In fact his history was so vanilla that I don't recall hardly any of it. Small town was supposed to lead to big college which in turn was supposed to lead to big city. Except that when he was in college, Silvio heard this story about the interstate system out in Los Angeles. He heard, or read, that the when the city planners were designing the highway out there in L.A. that they purposefully designed it to be inefficient—to be a pain in the ass for traffic. They thought that once people realized how much of a nightmare it is to commute that they'd all start carpooling and using public transportation, thus reducing the number of cars on the road and increasing the efficiency of the system and of the people. Instead, it was just a daily nightmare for all those commuters. Nobody carpooled. In fact, for a stretch of time, people in that area had the highest number of cars per person than anywhere else in the world. It was a disaster. Now, I don't exactly remember what that had to do with Silvio never moving to a big city, but I'm sure that that's the anecdote that he fed to me when he talked about returning to his home town. I guess Silvio doesn't like traffic. Or he doesn't like carpooling. I'm not sure really.

My recall for these particular moments wasn't hazy because I'm a bad listener, but because I was so focused on when the conversation would turn to the whole saint thing, I didn't process much else. And, the thing is, the conversation never really took that turn. I prodded him about it and asked questions with the hope that he'd expound on certain details of the whole enterprise, but he never did. He had this whole *what will be, will be* attitude about it, which I guess is pretty saintly and probably the best attitude to have about such a thing. He said there were hundreds of saints that I'd never even heard of—that most people had never heard of—but they were saints nonetheless. He didn't feel the need, in this lifetime, to be recognized as such. He said that he enjoyed the pursuit of it and the lifestyle of it more than anything else, even if he wasn't sure how long he could sustain what he was doing. It gave him clear and specific purpose. I nodded and said that I could appreciate that.

When he had to get on with his day we agreed to talk more at bingo that night, but before we left he said that he had one more thing he wanted to share. He asked me if I knew who Charlie Chaplin was and I said that of course I did. He told me that, back in the day, there was a Charlie Chaplin lookalike contest and, for good sport, Chaplin decided that he would enter into the contest. You know what happened next? Chaplin took third place in his own lookalike contest. Third place. There were two other guys just in this contest who were more Chaplin than Chaplin was. Silvio loved that. He said that the authentic versions of things were overrated and overvalued, and that often times the fake versions—the imposters—were higher quality than the originals. In their missions to be something they weren't, the imposters were the ones who took nothing for granted. They highlighted every trait they were supposed to have and downplayed everyone they weren't. Because they were outsiders, they knew how the originals were perceived *by* outsiders, and this advantage of perception allows the imposter to play to those perceptions. Silvio said he didn't have to be a saint as much as he had to be perceived as one. Then he laughed, gave a poorly executed wink, and headed back in the direction of the church. I just stood on the sidewalk in front of the diner and watched him go. An enigma in the fresh light of the morning. A wannabe saint, like no one I'd ever met.

I walked back to the storage unit and read in my copy of *The Rose of the Darkest Butte* until later that night.

Claims and Nature

The old man doesn't like it when I talk about death—he tells me that I'm supposed to leave thoughts like that to old timers like him.

Lewis nodded.

The two of them sat in a couple of steel fold-out chairs at the back of the gymnasium. Lewis picked half-heartedly at the paint job of the chair while the beige paint chips floated to the dust cover of the tile floor. The gym had low, exposed hanging steel rafters that no one ever cared to paint. All told, there were six basketball hoops that hung from the ceiling at the geometric base of apparent plumbing pipes. The backboards were made of cheap plywood and a thinly painted blue square donned the middle of each board. The rims had no springs and so any young athlete with the ability to dunk the basketball threated to tear down the dangling structures. There were old rubber and leather basketballs strung haphazard around the gym's floor, and Lewis sat with one of these on his lap as he picked at a leather flap that had begun to peel away from the ball's surface. The ball also had several malignant humps where people had kicked it or sat on it for too long. He ran his rough hand over the bulges and experimented with pushing them back to the level of the ball's primary sphere, but he could not. He cradled it in his lap and wrapped his arms around it as if in protection of a great egg. The several dozen bingo contestants, ranging from kind-of-old to very-old, occupied similar metal chairs along nine long fold out tables set in three rows. Vera called numbers from a podium at the front of the gym and only took her eyes off the two sitting in the back long enough to read the coded ping pong balls. Silvio slouched slightly in his chair with his feet ranging in front of him and a legal pad and pen grasped in his two hands on which he tracked the numbers that Vera called.

But I say that death isn't the elders' game, it's their inevitability—their looming, if not immediate future. What does someone in their great age have to fear from dying? Their gift has already been given to the world. Very often death offers them an escape—from regrets, from bodily pain, and from the disorientation of their senses that used to tell them how the world is. What is lost? All that these people can know of death is that they are ready for it. Don't you agree? It's the youth that are the real experts on the subject. Within us is where there is real loss in the act of dying. In us is an impressive potential, and though so many are apt to squander it, it is potential nonetheless. For the young to die is to kill the present, and the future. What's past is past. Decades of contributions lay ahead of us, and all of that could be wiped out in a car accident, or a rare disease, or an overdose of our own vices. The young are the real gamblers. They'll bet everyday they have ahead of them against a reckless night of drinking and a few cheap thrills. I'm not saying it's honorable or anything. And it's definitely not smart. But it's the young that are sitting down at the table with the high stakes and where the grim reaper always has a seat. How can we not think about death when our very essence and the future of that essence is at risk? You know? Maybe something truly special lies ahead of us, if only we can drag this heap of flesh to the point of realization. Isn't that funny? Isn't it the young that have everything to lose in death and yet are dually tasked and expected to pay it no attention? Tasked with their immortality and no one else's.

Silvio paused to write down the next number called over the microphone. His legal pad already had three columns of letter and number combinations written in dark pen with his spare handwriting. The first two columns were mostly blotted out by crosshatches and checkmarks, and the third had only a handful of archived numbers.

Then he said, That's why to me—and I mean no offense—war is the most evil of God's iterations. Because its old men sending young men to their deaths. It's the desecration by one generation of the next. Humans would be well served to do anything other than go to war. It is a veil behind which all manner of aggression can be orchestrated. Its very title echoes with the conviction that war is only undertaken by decent people trying to protect against war itself. The behavior of war in our species is its darkest stain. It is the medium through which cowards manipulate their paths to power, and the courageous are condemned to death. And death itself? Death is natural. Death is *meaningful*. But war is the manipulation of that meaning, because its victims are chosen arbitrarily from such a consequential population.

War is our greatest, most perverse evil. War is original sin. I pray deeply for you and everyone in it. There are more meaningful ways for one to die, and I hope your friend's death wasn't for nothing.

Lewis sat unresponsive except for a few discrete nods of his head. He continued to grip searchingly over the rough leather of the basketball. He looked at Silvio, trying to judge if he were going to say more, and when the silence lingered he said, I hope so too. But if he did die for anything, I can't figure what it is.

Silvio scratched another number onto his legal pad and said, Not everyone dies for something.

Lewis made a noticeable shift in his seat and Silvio's pen blotted the page where it stopped moving. Silvio said, I'm sorry. I didn't mean to imply that your friend's life was meaningless.

Silvio reached and patted Lewis on the near shoulder. There were thirty-four bingo players in attendance, which was a pretty good turnout by Silvio's estimation. On the west side of the gym, to the far right of where Vera called out numbers, was a concession stand that served Silvio's homemade chili out of two large crockpots. There were a handful of candy options too. There were no posted prices and customers were asked to only pay what they could, or what they thought was fair. There were saltine crackers and there was shredded cheese and at the end of the night Silvio stashed away the money that was made and either funneled it toward the rucksack project or plotted other ways that he could put it to use. Mounted high on the gym's wall behind Vera was a tin covered scoreboard that tracked the called numbers with columns and rows of white lights that hid under the milky round shells of fluorescent bulb coverings that had their corresponding bingo numbers painted on in a crude, black acrylic. There were spots where the electric heat of the lights burned through the bulbs' thin layering, and the tin covering was rusted and dented in spots where it had been hit by errant basketballs. The game was played with paper cards and marker pens that splotched their viscous ink in perfectly round globs on the targeted number. Silvio stared at nothing at all as he traced circles of various sizes into the air with his pen, like a sad magician who could summon miracles with the power of apathy. Vera eyed the two of them.

The funny thing is that I'd be terrified to go to war, but I'm not afraid to die. I'm just afraid to die *like that*, Silvio said.

You're not afraid to die?

That's right.

Have you ever seen somebody die?

Silvio stopped moving his pen hand and looked at the lights of the bingo scoreboard. He nodded his head as if he came to an agreement with some fleeting thought in his head. He said, I don't know.

Lewis said, That's typically something that somebody knows.

Silvio nervously drummed his pen on his pant-covered kneecap and said, I've seen it.

Lewis looked long at the portrait of Silvio's face but could read nothing there and when his curious eyes met with Vera's from across the gym, their glances quickly darted in separate directions.

Lewis asked, Well if you're not afraid of death, then what are you afraid of?

Besides war?

Besides that.

Silvio said, I'm afraid of a lot of things. A lot.

What's the biggest one?

The biggest one? That's a good question.

Silvio let out a quiet humming sound to signal that he was thinking. He tapped his pen on his legal pad and thought long enough that Vera had called three more numbers over her microphone. He recorded the numbers down in the same succession as the previous and he said, It's going to sound stupid . . . but my biggest fear is a thought. A thought about the edge of space. Not space itself. Not the size of it or all that cold and all that darkness. What I'm afraid of is that out there are millions of light years of galaxies and matter, and if you go far enough in any direction you're going to eventually reach the last thing that there is. That's the edge of space. And at that place is a planet or a star or a moon that is on the outermost margin of all existence. I'm afraid of what lays one step beyond that. That's my biggest fear.

That's it?

That's it. It's pretty dumb.

Lewis bounced the lopsided basketball in his hands once on the ground between his feet. He said, I don't think that any fear is dumb. But I am a little confused by it.

Silvio said, Shoot.

Well you're obviously a religious person, Lewis said. And so that place that you talked about. The edge. That's where god is, isn't it? That's heaven?

I guess that's one interpretation of it.

What's the other?

That it's the place where God stops.

A lady from across the gym called out her bingo to collective murmur of disappointment from the other players in the gym. She waved her card above her head with a large smile as she walked it toward Vera at the front. Silvio rose from this chair to meet the two at the front. He and Vera conferred with the lady's card and his legal pad and announced her card's legitimacy to another murmur of disappointment. The lady won twenty-seven dollars and she squeezed it in both hands as she strutted back to her seat and prepared a new card. Vera announced over the microphone that another game would be beginning shortly. Silvio took his seat next to Lewis again and crossed out the numbers from the previous game.

Sorry about that.

Lewis said, Not a problem.

Do you mind if I ask? Silvio said.

Ask what?

What your biggest fear is?

No.

What is it?

Dying.

Silvio nodded his head and said, What is it about dying that you find so scary?

Lewis shrugged. He said, I don't know. I'm afraid of the physical pain. I'm afraid that I don't know what happens afterward and I'm afraid that *nothing* happens afterward. Probably the biggest fear though is that I'll get down to those final moments and I'll come to a realization that my life wasn't anything worthwhile. That I wasted it.

Those are some unsettling thoughts.

Not for you.

Those thoughts unsettle me too. They just aren't the most unsettling ones that I can think of.

He motioned with his chin toward the general area of the players and said, People around here will probably agree with you though. They'll pray and they'll sing and they'll tell you all about the glories and the triumphs of heaven, and still when someone dies you wouldn't think that person was going anywhere nice at all. Maybe it's just a classic fear of the unknown, but I think it's also bigger than that. It's holding on to anything we can in this world because we have no idea what awaits us in the next one. I can't say that I do either, but I know that I'm not afraid of it. I'm not afraid of nothing either, if that's what it is. Sometimes one's death can amplify everything about their life—make the myth. The younger the person, the larger we see their potential, the bigger the myth becomes. Hendrix and Kennedy and that guy that the other guy wrote American Pie about—the day the music died. Dying made them immortal. And if not for fear of our existence after this one, then why hold on to the strands of mediocrity afforded to us here? Am I so great that this world can't get on without me? Isn't there a way that I can depart that will have more impact than all the days that I could stay?

Lewis wasn't sure if this question warranted an answer where the others didn't, and so he mumbled the words, I think so.

Silvio nodded and said, I think so too.

He scratched his arm. He said, I know so.

Silvio twisted his foot onto the tile floor, which brought out a series of quiet, rubbery squeaks that, for the two of them, cut into the concentrated quiet and lifeless tone of Vera's as she murmured on again at the microphone. B22, O64, N41, and so on. The wet sponges of the bingo markers—pink and yellow and blue—hovered over each sheet in preparation of the next square to be blotched. Marked and dismissed. Reading glasses and squinting eyes. That young gal who calls the numbers is so quiet. What was that number she just called? I69? An obligatory whoop of appreciation—an ex-soldier chuckles. The money of the game all going, in small amounts of pleasure, to the likes of Frank and Leroy and Jeanette and Edna and Theodore and Christine. Like a retirement fund for people who are the last of their names. The world is different now, Agnes, you can't say that anymore. Discontent of the old soul who blames time for being out of touch when they never had anything figured out in the first place, and you can't lose what you never had.

Cedric never wins. He has been coming to bingo every Monday night for sixteen years and he has never won once. He throws away another failed card—another ticket unpunched—and leans over to his de facto friend, Kenneth, and says to him, I hate this damn game. Lost again. That gal that calls the numbers sure does have a nice ass though, eh there Ken? And Kenneth rolls his eyes because he knows that Cedric never wins because he can't see anything and he can't hear anything. He just likes pressing the wet markers into the paper and creating the myth of himself as the man who hasn't gotten a single bingo in sixteen years. The world's unluckiest man. All of Kenneth's friends are dead, and so he has Cedric. But that girl who calls the numbers sure has a nice ass, am I right? B19.

I know it, Lewis. I know that this is what I was called to do. Sainthood. This is my purpose, *my* meaningful life.

Something surged within Silvio that seemed to be contained only by the soles of his shoes and the beaten rubber stoppers on the legs of the chair. He, like a fleeting and unharnessed bolt of lightning just burning to be witnessed. A moment of pure energy gone to waste on the unwitnessed strike of a tree that stands unattended in nature. Future travelers will see a history of the moment in the tree's scarred bark and admire the power of the lightning and resilience of the wood. Such a collision of forces, but only one among many.

Look, they'll say. There's a rock that's been split in half by the persistence of freezing water. Incredible.

The ex-soldier looked upon him, the saint, with wide eyes. Who among mortal men was he? How had the death of one great heart led him so miraculously to the next? Was it some duty of his, some destiny, to bear witness to these men, the forgotten? Or did he play a role more crucial than even that—to forge the story as well as to tell it? The difference, no difference—he, lord of it all.

Across the gymnasium came the frail voice of some player's claim to bingo.

Silvio Submission Twelve:

PREFACE

It is the flash of lightning that contains all of the dazzling power—
the one moment where gods and men recognize each other
for what they are and everything else takes place under our feet.

There is only the lightning—
the lightning and our search for the faces behind it.

As the Rain Falls

God sends his only son to the earth. While he is here he has a crown of thorns compressed into his skull, he is lashed to near death, stabbed, and nailed to a piece of wood while he's still alive. If that can happen to God's son, how do you figure there won't be any suffering?

I guess I just thought that he went through all of that so we didn't have to suffer.

My friend, he went through all of that to show us *how* to suffer. What if someone did all of that to your son?

Lewis filled both of his cheeks with air and let out a quick exhale before he said, There'd be hell to pay.

Their voices traveled quietly in the cold fall air. They were supported by the hard aluminum of the baseball field bleachers where the diamonds had been all but abandoned since the beginning of school and their infields already housed newly sprouted weeds. They were alone in the park, and though the sun shone on them as it did every other day, it gave them no warmth. It was just a star so far away and they were just the cooled beings born from its cousin's dust—dust that once swirled and condensed into an iron alloy core not very different from the iron core of the hemoglobin that fueled the likes of these two creatures that looked on the setting sun and wondered why it wasn't warm enough. Then the saint wondered if they weren't all just made on the dust-blown bones of fallen gods, and if they were then what gods watched now and what kinds of ends awaited *them?*

Is Vera more than a friend to you?

It's not like that.

A quiet baseball field and its weeded pitcher's mound. A garden of flowers pulled toward the cold sun while the season's first frost climbs their stalks. Vast deserts where the viscous remains of dinosaurs and time lurk under the sand in great swaths of black oceans that are burned and spewed by those that dream about them. A relic battlefield where the fallen only prayed that the dust of their death could be as the death of the gods that birthed them. The mortar and brick of churches and the hidden pores of their lawns that only needed the rain to unlock the scent.

Did you kill anybody?

I don't know. I really don't. I just fired my gun and hoped not to die. That's all it was.

The soldier and a palm of lives cast into the desert wind with nobody to ferry the guilt of their taking. Snuffed out by the wavering barrel of a gun manned by a ghost. Typical ghost behavior. Part of him wishes he would have aimed, and the other part knows that he'd probably be dead if he did. He dreamt of the roaring jet engines that brought death from above and he dreamt of his friend, and when he tried to picture his friend's face he could only see the half of it that caved in. He dreamt about the seas of oil and he dreamt about the bad guys, and they were all in the desert but he didn't know where. It began to rain and it was a cold rain.

Silvio said, What did Jude die for?

He didn't die for anything.

What if he could?

What if he could what?

Die for something important. Die with meaning.

Hypothetically?

Yes.

I think it'd help. It'd make it better. I don't know. He'd still be dead.

Would you give it to him? Would you give him that meaningful death?

I wouldn't give him any death.

What if you had to?

Why would I have to?

To save him.

He thought he understood but he was too afraid to clarify. Would his face be in his dreams as well? He wondered how long dreams stayed and what he could do to make them go away. Behind their bleacher was a park that was every bit as empty as the baseball fields, and behind that was a neighborhood of single story houses with gable roofs and asphalt shingles whose cheap thinness provided little protection from the extreme weather of the summers and winters. Rising over the lip of one of the houses was the grey entrails of cigarette smoke that she carelessly blew into the frozen air as if the she were the one that supplied the sky's clouds from her flushed lips. She breathed deeply and smelled the air with a raised nose as an animal does. It was made tight by the cold, and when she smelled it all she could smell was the temperature. The amber wavelengths from the dying sun played off her healthy skin and her smoking hand no longer shook when she took a drag, as it had in months past. She heard the rain before she felt it. It pattered over her house's roof and on the porch around her and then the cold drops made contact with the skin exposed on her smoking hand. She coolly took a final drag from it and flicked its filtered end into a ceramic flower pot that lined the back porch of the house. It was nearly filled by cigarette butts, but in the other handful of pots was the evidence of her summer hobby, and the flowers bloomed vibrantly in the face of the approaching cold. She squatted in front of one and grabbed its stem as she had seen the saint do and she looked at it briefly before going inside and closing the door behind her.

The saint turned on his bleacher seat in response to what he thought was a distant door closing. He remarked how strange it was to be so cold at this time of year and his companion responded by tucking his hands into the open-bottom jacket that he had bought at the truck stop that morning. Despite living out of a storage shed and a truck stop for nearly two weeks, the soldier still appeared in better condition than his counterpart, whose devout fasting had taken all of the color and weight out of his face.

How do you know you've done enough?

There are many who've done less.

But what about you?

It's not up to me. And if it was just about how much one gives, then only rich people would be in heaven.

Maybe you should keep working.

How many have you met like me?

Why do you want this?

The old man rode his strangled gait a quarter of the way up the hill before he stopped moving. His legs were shaking and he dropped his hands to his knee caps to steady them while he caught his shallow breath. He still had a few hundred feet of asphalt to go if he wished to make it to the top, and he looked at it for a long while as his breath quieted. It was the same hill he used to perch on and admire the small town's absent skyline, and it was the same hill that the saint would hike in order to chase storms across the horizon. The old man used to chase storms too, but with his inability to conquer the hill came the inability to chase the storm. Trapped in the bowl of the valley, all he could do was look upward at the clouds' albescent underbelly. He thought it looked like it carried snow, but he couldn't remember the last time it had snowed this early in the year. After another look to the summit, he tentatively balanced his way back down the hill's minor slope and cut a path south through a neighborhood not unlike the one around the church that he spent so much time at. It began to rain and he pulled a wool cap out of his jacket's front pocket and stretched its loose fibers over his empty scalp. When he walked in his front door he was met by the smell of freshly baked cinnamon rolls and his wife gave him a hug and asked him how his walk was. The years and her degraded posture had shrunk her below the five foot mark and so she needed his help in reaching for a specific set of Tupperware. She asked him how the saint was doing and the old man said that he was worried. She told him not to be. She hugged him again and forced a cinnamon roll into his hand and told him the game had already started. He walked into the bomb-shelter advertisement of their living room and took a seat in a pumpkin colored rocking chair that was worn out where his hands and feet rested the most. She came in a minute later with a roll of her own and sat in an identical chair. She was wearing a faded baseball cap and she told him that this was the best time of the year for baseball and he said that he couldn't agree more. The rain tapped at their living room window like a restless finger and he used a wooden lever to kick his chair back into a reclined position. He rested his hands on his chest like one does inside a coffin and by the fourth inning he was in a deep sleep. She covered him with a wool blanket and finished watching the game while she worked on a large cross-stitch of rose. The game ended and, unwilling to wake him, she turned off the television and went to bed in the other room while the darkness settled in around him. He dreamt of the Iowa cornfields of his youth. He dreamt of baseball parks where the outfields were sodded with Kentucky bluegrass and that he tended the grass on the back of a John Deere 4320. Then he dreamed that he was in a garden with the saint and when he asked him to climb a nearby hill, the old man said that he could not. The saint started walking up the hill and the old man watched him from the garden. He walked high and far away and when he turned around he held a rifle in his hand. He pointed it and aimed at the old man and smiled. The old man woke up in the dark living room, and he was very afraid.

Winter Cells

The atmosphere above the town churned and rolled slowly and soundlessly. As the dull tint of the sun graced other provinces it left behind here a dark and cold reality. In the unconsidered night it swirled back upon itself until it formed a thick and gray mass that settled inside the valley. The weight of the thing alone seemed to compress and slow all time beneath it. For a time the rain disappeared, as if retreated to gather its strength, and the atmosphere it left behind was dry and quiet. Leaves still hung from the branches of trees and its cold was uncanny. Not many were awake when the white mass began to sprinkle immense snow-flakes through their condensed time and onto the world, but those that were could appreciate their quiet tumble into the relatively-warm oblivion of the turf below. For a time the flakes vanished, leaving behind the damp surface of the earth as the only proof of their passing, but surely they set in on the doomed histories of the fallen before them—pelting the remembrance of the sun's work until it was buried beneath the winter that is now.

She was one who watched. Her hands were tucked into the pockets of her pajamas and she admired the flakes sway and settle within the coned luminescence of the street light while the sound of the bathtub's faucet echoed from the other room. She undressed herself as she walked down the house's hallway and took in the environment of the bathroom before entering—the soft light of the candles and the thin veil of moisture that clasped to the window as if to shield her from the frozen cage outside. The metal clink of the razorblade she laid on the edge of the tub reverberated loudly around the hard porcelain cell as she cut the faucet and stepped into the steaming water. It was so quiet without the pour of the water that she thought she could hear each individual snowflake outside fall into place among its kin. Too quiet. She used her foot to turn the handle of hot water back on and lowered her head into the noisy depths of the glass tub and its private waterfall.

He sat awake in the cavity of her dead husband's past. He could hear the water drip off the tin roof but took it to be a light rain, unaware of the white weight that gathered on his tin shelter. There wasn't much sleep to be had in his mind. He spent most of the night sitting on the futon with his elbows on his knees and his flashlight pinned between his feet and shining under his chin like the teller of some nightmare that can only be shared in the company of a campfire. He played through his journey as best as he could and looked into his future, but he could determine nothing. He thought about Jude and he thought about Silvio. He thought about how Vera had not wanted to meet him when Silvio offered a more formal rendezvous between the two. He was nothing more than a walking dedication to the death of her lover. He was the authentic witness to the end of her world and living proof of her metaphorical death. He mulled over the theme of destiny that was so prevalent in the fantasy books of his past and it gave him little comfort. Whether everything had been laid out millennia before his birth, or each moment was called forth from a limitless nonexistence, it couldn't change where he'd been and what he had to go through to be here. None who drove by the tin storage units could have guessed they were haunted by a war-veteran turned Atropos. And though he didn't know what spun the thread, or what measured its length, he found himself with the abhorred shears and he questioned the sanity of his promotion. He moved the space heater toward the foot end of the futon and bit the flashlight in his mouth as he prepared himself for sleep. He lay with his feet toward the back of the storage unit and propped his head on the padded arm of the futon. The flashlight still hung in his mouth like a bloated cigarette, and before he clicked it off it lingered over the rifle propped in the opposite corner of the compartment. That was the final image of which he seen and which he dreamed.

The saint glided through the snowflakes with his hood raised against the endless sky of stars that hid behind the thick clouds. He crossed an empty field and approached the small wood shed that was marked by a soft gilded light that glowed like a covered candle in the dark night. He stopped several feet outside of the light that came from the shed's unfastened door and he looked around the dark countryside as the flakes that melted against his body heat already settled several inches deep onto the ground. He moved in on the shed's cracked door and it painted a rectangle of light down his approaching figure. All that was left of the door's former handle were two splintered screw holes and so he used his bare hand to pull it further open by the door's lock stile. The bottom of the door scraped along the dirt base until it caught on a small rise of frozen soil that had built up from previous entries. He pulled back his hood as he stepped into the light and he was met by a dozen sets of anxious eyes.

None of the cats blinked or moved a muscle as he oriented himself in their small hovel. They were packed into the far left corner, opposite of where he entered, and in the other far corner was the space heater whose searing orange heated coils provided some measure of heat to the room. In the corner nearest to where he entered was a small electric lamp set on top of the cat's food storage. The cats were stacked and entangled in their corner and he thought their suspicious eyes were on him as he cut into a new bag of food. Then he cut a hole into all of the remaining bags. When he turned around to face the cats again he realized that they were not watching him at all. Instead their eyes were on the dark and unclaimed corner of the shed where he could see a conspicuous lump on the ground. When he moved toward it, the on-looking cats lowered their heads and raised their shoulder blades and tensed against each other in anticipation. He crouched to get a better view of the dead kitten and when he reached out to touch it he was startled by a sharp hiss that came from the far corner. He looked at the crowd of cats and they were quiet again and he looked back at the white hairless form of the kitten. Its skin was cold to the touch and it didn't appear to ever have opened its eyes to the world. It was no bigger than the palm of his hand and the cats hissed again when he scooped up the tiny figure. He cupped it in one hand and grabbed a steel spade from behind the food bags, and then pushed the shed door closed as he entered back into the night. He held the spade in one hand and with the other he cradled the kitten delicately against his chest. A dozen paces from the shed he stopped and dropped to his knees. Even from a distance the outer lights of the hospital provided sparse vision in the field. He cupped the kitten in two hands and pressed the backs of his hands into the snow to create a small indent in which he laid the corpse. Far removed from the dens of its evolution. He directed his attention to the snowy ground in front of him that he cleared with his forearms and then used the spade to pick at the wet and frozen soil beneath. He swung the spade in small downward arcs and pulled at the loose earth in a rowing motion until a he had shaped a shallow grave. Again he used both of his hands to raise the cat from its depressed snow and set it in the awaiting tomb. His hands were uncovered, but he didn't seem to mind as he used them to fill the grave back in over the ghostly form of the kitten. He raised his shoulders and pressed on the ground with open palms as if the soil was the dough of this misplaced baker. He finished flattening the earth and then rose from his knees with wet pant legs and he looked around the field for something to mark the grave with. There was nothing and he tried momentarily to shove the handle end of the spade into the ground but he could not. He placed his hands on his hips and stood over the spot while the snow continued to cover the land. After the gravesite had been disguised again by the falling snow he walked back to the shed and propped the spade near the entrance of the door. He stepped inside again briefly to catch some of the shed's warmth and he noticed that the cats had spread out again to occupy the corner that was previously vacated by the dead kitten. They crawled over each other and licked themselves and they paid him no attention this time. He stood in front of the space heater and rubbed his hands ardently before heading back outside.

The atmosphere remained mute and heavy as he made his way out of the field and back toward the heart of the small town. All night the snow fell and it settled on the houses and in the streets. In the countryside it filled in the tilled rows of the empty cornfields first and then over the rest of it, until only the decapitated stalks stuck out from the snow like a former blast radius beset by a nuclear winter. At the east end of the town he scaled the hill so familiar to him and he heard the voice of an old friend telling him to go for the storms, but to stay for the stars. When he reached its apex he could see neither. It was him and the dull white suffocation of the falling flakes. They engulfed his pensive figure and he got lost in them as one does in a dream. The last night on earth for how many people and where did they all go when they departed? An answer to every mystery He carries or some other plane forged of this one? Whole histories melted into the next. More snowflakes out in the deep of the dark and the cold rest of the legions who have gone before.

Silvio Submission Thirteen:

FOOTPRINTS IN THE SAND

There are only my footprints here,
And the tide is rising.

I'm talking to myself and the tide is
growing stronger and I want
him to call out to me but I
only hear myself and I hear the
tide and I can't hear him call
out to me—if he is.

I hope he is somewhere watching
and calling for me, but why can't I hear him?
The tide is so loud.
Why am I so loud with fear of
the tide that I am not even
my own companion, and the tide is no companion
and I cannot hear him—
why can't I hear him?

I wish he would walk with me.
My footprints are here but they are alone.
I am not even my own companion.

My footprints are alone and they are not safe.
The tide is rising.

An American Tragedy?

They came down the snow trodden street like dust bowl refugees who had taken a wrong turn. Furniture dangled off the beds of the trucks and trailers in all manner of ornament, held on by ratchet straps and bungee cords and the arms of men and women bundled against the cold autumn wind. They entered as a line of six into the parking lot of the church and wordlessly began unloading the tangled goods onto old tarps and rugs. The snow was deep and already the morning sun had burned its way through the milky cloud above and caused the snow to become dense and heavy as it reflected the light into the eyes of the workers from all angles—each flake like a fragile mirror. They shoveled and kicked at the drifts with their feet to clear space on the pavement and before long nearly all the hardware from his parents' old house adorned the parking lot as if it were an interminable living room. Silvio was there, wiping down the wooden dressers and bookcases and desks and chairs, occasionally giving each a kick to determine its sturdiness. Quietly more people made their way through side streets and alleyways and into the lot where they admired and appraised each piece. They'd take their gloves off to feel at discolorations and scars at the wood and nod their approval to whoever they were with, if anyone. The scrape of wood drawers and the quiet impact of brass handles sounded in the white urban clearing.

Silvio took his place on a large landscape boulder near the intersection of where the church's lawn met the hard concrete of the lot and began the auction with the disclaimer that all proceeds would go directly to the church's rucksack project. He wore only jeans and a light jacket and his hands and ears burned red in their exposure to the cold. He didn't have the appropriate gab of a real auctioneer, but as he called up each item he gave its history or some anecdote concerning its value. Audience members used their eyes and their minds to measure up how each item might best conform to their place of living. They pictured which piece would best fit their favorite vacation knickknacks and jewelry dishes. They counted armoire drawers and compared their number against the inventory of bed sheets and towels they needed storage for. They took stock of the wood's hue and dismissed perfectly suitable stands and tables because their grain didn't fit, thematically, with the rest of the house. He wondered if certain pieces would go unclaimed. Maybe they'd eventually be crushed and cast out to use as fire wood, and so what? Did Prometheus, bound, endure that rock and that eagle for naught? Furniture should be so lucky to find that fate, he thought.

Across the street, the front and backyard of her house was connected by an un-fenced strip of lawn that ran alongside the house between her and her neighbor, and it is along this that he crept and then laid prone. Great heaves of frozen air came from his mouth as he tried to catch his breath from his run across town and through alleyways, dodging cars and pedestrians alike. It's not simple or subtle to cross town unseen with a rifle in one's hands. He didn't bother with the scope because he didn't have the opportunity to sight it in, and though he had beads of sweat running from his forehead, he quickly grew cold lying in the snow in his truck-stop attire. Never mind, he'd only be there for a few minutes.

She was there too, quiet like she was. She had no interest in the furniture for auction and only looked at him upon his rock, a body above all else and doing what form of good he knew how. Across the street a For Sale sign hailed from her front lawn and signaled more desires for her than to simply sell a house. Somewhere a new life waited for her, maybe better than the last. He was fluid and efficient and he had peddled off nearly a dozen items before a reflected glint of sunlight caught his eye from across the street. He tried to make out the source of the reflection but the snow on the ground gave off such a glare that he was left squinting into the white abyss. He raised an open hand to his brow in an attempt to shield his eyes but it gave him no relief.

He turned his gaze back to the mass of buyers as he dropped his hand from his forehead. They looked up at him from their position in the snow and they waited for him to announce the next piece up for auction. But he didn't say anything concerning the available furniture. He raised up both arms in a gesture that looked like a half shrug and he said,

It is finished.

The blast of the shot was one that had never resounded in the neighborhood before that morning. Its loud clap and resounding thunder seemed to wipe all fond memories and noises of the area into a dead silence—no noisy kids in the street and no family barbeques and no Sunday chats on the way into the church. It was a sound so foreign that none in the lot knew what to make of it. The old man wasn't sure he had heard anything and Vera had her head ducked slightly with her hands clasped over her ears, looking for the source of the noise. All seemed normal and mostly it was, except for Silvio's absence from the rock. She pushed through the idle and confused crowd toward where he should be, but she couldn't know what she was going to find there—who could?

Silvio lay heaped atop the cold earth with his lifeblood and the remnants of a thirty-ought-six shell scattered on the snow covered lawn behind him. The red of his blood streaked on the white like some violent enactment of the Milky Way's beauty, and he didn't let out so much as a gasp. His fading and panicked eyes made out Vera's crying face as she screamed at the people around her for help, but there was nothing to be done. Who was she screaming about? Who was Jude? Wasn't his name Silvio? In the wild searching of his final moments he found the face of the old man sitting in quiet shock on the stone where he stood just moments before. The gazes of the dying men locked, and though a primitive fear still shone in his eyes, his final breath brought with it an imperceptible smile.

I once was an ant. I nearly died to a hotdog. I murdered a good man to make him a better one. I don't know what one has to believe in order to believe these things, but I do. If two men fight over conflicting ideals, the loser never changes his mind about his ideals, only about who he should fight over them. Take it from me, I used to be a soldier.

I heard later that Silvio had arranged for everything he owned to be donated to the church in the event of his passing. However, he had made no burial arrangements, and when his body was cremated the old man had his remains placed in an urn and on top of the empty pedestal that sat in the church's garden—the pedestal that Silvio said he wanted to adorn but never did. I left the gun where it was fired and stuffed a rolled up envelope into the trigger guard on which I wrote, *Christianity Sucks*. I thought that note would help with the whole martyr business, and maybe the fact that he was killed by a dead man's gun from the very house that said dead man used to live, then maybe that could count as a miracle—probably not, but I'm not the one who decides those things. I was back to the storage unit and then to the truck stop in a matter of minutes because I'd never run so fast in my life. I was lucky enough to catch a semi heading west in just a few minutes and back on the road I went. I don't know if they're looking for me, but they can get in line behind the United States Army because I'm not an easy one to find. They'll have to tear this country to its foundations before they ever find me, reading some generic Western under the shelter of an interstate overpass, flashlight clenched in my teeth. Endless skies above me but I pay them no attention—not until a world ender of a storm comes heading my way. Good luck.

When strangers pick up this hitchhiking soldier and tell him their histories, I'll have one of my own this time. I'd tell them about how I had met a saint—a real life saint. Silvio, they'd say. That's Italian, right?

Each bolt that powered through the sky reminded me of Silvio. And Jude. Temporary and brilliant. Unseen and unremembered by most. Not me though. Because when the storms cleared out to reveal the stars above, well those reminded me of them too.

The stars themselves aren't important. They sit as indifferent objects ready to be admired by the next ant, the next dead soldier, the next martyr. After all, what is a single star? It only becomes important when it's part of a constellation of which it doesn't know its place anyway. It glows as the eye of this earthly creature, the belt buckle of that forgotten hero, or the symbol of hope that shone its way through the clouds and the smoke. But what if your perspective shifted? I wonder what lost objects and forgotten creatures you could witness on the surface of those ethereal giants. Suddenly you don't give a shit that you're on the belt buckle because the belt buckle can't exist when you're sitting on it. It was born of perspective and now it dies by it.

But it wouldn't be all that bad. You could draw your own invisible lines, create your own constellations, name them after family members, pets, childhood heroes, and so on. And if you spend enough time looking you might be able to locate our own sun with all that new perspective. You might decide it's actually the eye of some strangely familiar face, or just a face that is strange. But you wouldn't be able to see this dark planet orbiting that place of light, and you certainly could not identify me, riding the slow spin—walking along the highway and somehow not being pitched into space.